It was a night
for discovery

"Shy? You though[t] ... [voice]
broke as he lost a[nd] ... [pulling]
Chandra toward him, he bent her
backward over his arm and kissed
her boldly.

Chandra's senses reeled as she felt the
strength of his desire. His hands moving
masterfully over her body made it difficult
for her to think clearly. Finally, as his
mouth teased the sensitive spot behind
her ear, she moaned, "Okay, okay!
I take it back—"

"Too late," he interrupted, his warm breath
causing a sensuous flurry against her skin.
"Lady, you've got a lot to learn...."

THE AUTHOR

Jenna Lee Joyce is one of the pen names
used by two friends who live eight blocks
apart in Columbus, Ohio. Also known as
Janet Joyce, they have collaborated on
many romances, both contemporary and
historical. Neither of them can conceive
of a time when they'll stop working
together. They say with a chuckle,
"We've worn such a path between our
two houses, the city may start assessing
us for street improvement!"

Books by Jenna Lee Joyce

HARLEQUIN TEMPTATION
39–WINTERSFIELD
59–CROSSROADS

These books may be available at your local bookseller.

Don't miss any of our special offers. Write to us at the
following address for information on our newest releases.

Harlequin Reader Service
P.O. Box 52040, Phoenix, AZ 85072-2040
Canadian address: P.O. Box 2800, Postal Station A,
5170 Yonge St., Willowdale, Ont. M2N 6J3

Crossroads

JENNA LEE JOYCE

Harlequin Books

TORONTO • NEW YORK • LONDON
AMSTERDAM • PARIS • SYDNEY • HAMBURG
STOCKHOLM • ATHENS • TOKYO • MILAN

Published May 1985

ISBN 0-373-25159-9

1

EVENTUALLY the annoying drone became so loud that Chandra Collins could no longer ignore it. This was the third morning in a row she'd been awakened by the same irritating noise. Bleary-eyed, she stared at the alarm clock on the nightstand, then issued an exasperated groan. Five A.M.! No civilized human being should be forced out of bed at such an ungodly hour, especially on a weekend. Where was that sound coming from? A boat? A car? A chain saw? Whatever, she'd had enough.

No matter how unappealing the prospect, she was going to get up, get dressed and give whoever was making a habit of disturbing her sleep a good piece of her mind. This was the last day of her hard-earned, three-day vacation and some unfeeling moron had ruined it, rousting her out of bed at the crack of dawn. She rubbed the sleep from her dark brown eyes, then pushed a wild tangle of sable-colored curls off her forehead. Tentatively, she slid one long leg then the other out of the warm bed until her toes touched the planked floor. The varnished wood was just as cold as it had been every morning since she'd arrived at the cabin.

It was late July, but already the nights in the Arrowhead section of northern Minnesota were cool and the mornings crisp. If it wasn't for that imbecile outside, she'd have been able to stay in bed until the sun warmed things up a bit. *Like about noon,* she thought darkly.

"I'm going to get you for this," she warned out loud to the unseen trespasser. She stood shivering in the loft, shaking her fist at the triangular glass that enclosed the front of the A-frame cabin.

She pulled on a pair of jeans, a sweat shirt and her canvas shoes to the accompaniment of the now familiar whine that increased to a nerve-racking growl then diminished to a sputter only to increase in volume and pitch again. By the time she stumbled to the front door of the cabin and stepped outside onto the redwood deck, her anger had reached mammoth proportions. Even though she'd been out of her soft warm bed for only a few minutes, she had a scathing speech all rehearsed.

Willow Lake was located in an isolated patch of wilderness surrounded by thick forest. Except for the small acreage owned by her caretaker, Henry Raincloud, the land on all sides was Collins property. Henry was a full-blooded Chippewa Indian who made his living as a guide. During hunting and fishing season he had Chandra's authorization to take parties out on her land, but motorcycles had never been mentioned in any of the semiannual reports he had sent her. The man was nearly seventy years old, hardly an age to take up motorcycle riding. It certainly wasn't Henry destroying her solitude so who the devil was it?

Trying to locate the intended victim of her wrath, she scanned the area. The noise seemed to be coming from below her. She leaned over the wooden rail and looked down the steep hill toward the lake. Her view was partly obstructed by the tall spruce and pines that grew up on the hill but she was gratified when the early-morning sun glinted off metal. In the next second, through a gap in the trees, she caught a glimpse of a fast-moving motorcycle and rider before they again disappeared behind a massive granite boulder.

A winding, dirt road led to the cabin but there were no other roads. Whoever was driving the motorcycle had to be following the old logging trail that angled up from the shores and over the ridge behind the cabin. Either that or the driver was forging a virgin path through the trees, and that would not only be the epitome of gall but virtually impossible. Only a fool would attempt to ride a motorcycle over such treacherous ground.

If she hurried, she might be able to cut him off as he took the sharp curve in the trail that lay a few yards away from the bottom steps to the cabin. Then she could deliver her tirade before the foolhardy rider killed himself. She hadn't left a warm bed at five o'clock in the morning only to confront a corpse.

Once she'd told him he could go commit suicide on somebody else's property, she'd crawl back into bed for several more hours of well-earned rest. She'd spent the past six months unraveling the complex finances of a floundering computer business in Minneapolis and hadn't had a decent night's sleep in that whole time. Spending three uninterrupted days in the isolated wilderness of Willow Lake was supposed to be her R and R before the start of her next assignment, a month-long audit at Hammond Paper Products.

She had reached the wide earthwork landing carved out of the hill about halfway down when she got her first clear view of her quarry. Looking below her, she had spotted the grooves his machine had made in the strip of wet sand along the shoreline. By following the tire marks, she had located the motorcycle churning up the logger's trail. The dark-clad rider was too far away for her to make her voice heard over the roar of the dirt bike's engine and besides, as soon as she saw what he was planning to do, the only sound she could manage was a shocked croak.

There was a natural ramp formed by a flat shelf of dark granite that protruded at a slight angle out over the cove. Chandra was sure the distance between the rock ledge and the drop to the opposite shore was almost fifty feet. The foolish daredevil was preparing to jump over the water! "Who does he think he is? Evel Knievel?" she muttered under her breath.

She could sense the determination in him even though his face was hidden behind the tinted visor of a fiberglass helmet. Wearing a brown leather jacket, leather pants and knee-high boots, he was outfitted like a seasoned biker, but Chandra still thought he was crazy to risk such a dangerous jump. *I've got to stop him! Probably some rash punk out to prove his manhood*, she judged. Surely no reasonable adult would contemplate doing something so incredibly stupid.

She waved her arms in the hope that he'd see her on the landing but all his concentration was centered on the responsive machine underneath him. His gloved hands twisted on the handlebars as he gunned the engine. The ominous growl increased in volume and the massive black motorcycle instantly answered the commands of its reckless rider and surged forward.

Chandra's arms dropped weakly to her sides as she watched the powerful bike career at top speed up the granite ramp, then launch into space. Like a huge mechanical bird, the motorcycle flew over the placid inlet. "Geronimo!" the rider shouted as he sailed through the air.

The bike thudded to a heavy landing on the wide sandy beach. The whole thing was over in seconds, bike and rider once again safe on solid ground, but Chandra couldn't move. Her heart was beating like a conga drum and her stomach was in knots as she clung to the landing rail, staring down at the lunatic who had just scared her half out of her wits.

Her speech was going to include not only an order to vacate the premises but also a stern lecture on personal safety. The rider wasn't just a menace to her and her property but to himself. If he had a death wish, fine, but she didn't want to witness anything as heart-stopping as that jump ever again in her life. She was still having a hard time believing he hadn't injured himself when he pulled off his helmet and gave her all the proof she needed.

Laughing uproariously, he tossed back his head, and droplets of sweat flew away from his light brown hair. Even from a distance, Chandra could see the excitement and triumph flashing in eyes as blue and fathomless as the late-summer sky. His mouth was slanted in a grin of pure male satisfaction. "Way to go, hotshot!" he asserted in an enthusiastic drawl, then raised one fist over his head in a gesture of supreme victory.

Damned fool kid! He won't be so pleased with himself when I get through with him, Chandra resolved, as she rapidly continued her descent down the wide steps. Even though she made no attempt to silence her approach, he didn't appear to be aware of her presence on the hill behind him. With easy nonchalance, he swung one leg over the seat of the motorcycle and stood away from the bike.

He was lean and intimidatingly tall, and for a moment Chandra hesitated. On closer inspection she saw that he wasn't a senseless teenager with something to prove but a mature man who looked to be well past thirty. Dressing down some thoughtless postadolescent boy was one thing but laying into a full grown male of the species was quite another. What if he was an over-the-hill member of some ruthless motorcycle gang who'd been born to raise hell? A bit more wary, Chandra elected to stay where she was and watch him for a few minutes before deciding whether or not to risk giving him her lecture.

The man stowed his helmet behind the seat of the bike, then placed his hands on his hips and gazed out over the lake. He strode purposefully toward the water but came to a halt before his boots encountered the foamy waves gently lapping the shore. Balancing himself on one leg, he pulled off a boot and a sock, then switched legs and removed his remaining footgear. He was careful to place the expensive leather boots well away from the water. Evidently the man did have some sense of value, Chandra decided. Even if he'd shown a marked disrespect for her property, it appeared he had some respect for his own.

It was hard not to laugh when he danced a little jig, then dug his bare toes into the sand. Using his big toe, he drew something on the wet beach but without getting considerably closer, Chandra couldn't make it out. How many times had she done that very same thing when she was a little girl vacationing here? He might be a man but his antics resembled those of a carefree boy. She felt her defenses lower a notch. Even so, she stepped behind the leafy branches of a young birch growing beside the bottom step so she could continue watching him without being seen.

Bending down, the man picked up a flat stone and skipped it over the surface of the water. Again and again, he arced his arm and hurled the missiles with great force until one sank beneath the waves as soon as it hit, spoiling his perfect record.

"Nuts!" he bellowed, then childishly kicked at the sand with his bare foot. Jamming his hands into the pockets of his supple leather jacket, he shrugged his wide shoulders and started walking toward the old weather-beaten dock that jutted out from the shore.

Chandra smiled in amusement and relief. A man who used the word "nuts" instead of a more explicit comment on his personal failure would be drummed out of any self-respecting, lawless gang. He might ride his motorcycle with rash abandon and dress like a Hell's Angel but she was no longer worried about his reaction to her wholly justified complaints.

Bypassing the ramshackle boat house, Chandra was less than ten yards behind him when he started undressing. In seconds, he had stripped off both the brown jacket and the white T-shirt he wore underneath and dropped them onto the dock. An instant later, he pulled down the wide zippers on each side of his leather pants.

At the first sight of his bare behind, crisscrossed by two wide elastic straps, Chandra had become rooted to the ground. When she was given a full display of his naked backside, she swiftly uprooted herself and ducked around the corner of the boat house. She could hardly confront him now. Then again, he certainly deserved a shock equal to the one he'd given her with that foolhardy jump over the cove.

Under the present circumstances, if she strode out on the dock and stated her grievances against him, she could almost guarantee she'd never see hide nor hair of him again. She muffled an amused giggle in her hand. Now that would be a pity, for all the hide and hair she'd seen thus far was gorgeous. She couldn't help herself and peeked out for another look.

All she saw was a flash of golden skin above the fine white mist that rose up from the lake before the man dived beneath the surface of the water. She shivered at the sight, remembering how cold the water was before the heat of the day took the edge off. Since the lake was spring-fed, even on the hottest days the water temperature didn't rise much above sixty degrees. She recalled the many times in her childhood when she wouldn't be persuaded to wait to jump in until the afternoon and had had to suffer the subsequent cramps for her impatience.

This man was a real glutton for punishment. First

he brutally abused his body with that bone-jarring ride over rough terrain, vaulted out into space and landed with the force of a ton of rocks, then dived headfirst into a lake full of frigid water. She wondered what was next on his agenda. Perhaps skydiving into a ring of flames?

As the moments passed and he didn't surface, Chandra grew frightened. She stepped away from the boat house and moved closer to the beach, standing behind a large moss-covered rock as she stared into the lake. What if the shock of the cold water hitting his hot, sweat-drenched skin had been too much for him? What if he'd sunk to the bottom just like that stone he'd tossed? Or been paralyzed by an intense cramp?

For the second time in a matter of minutes, Chandra felt sure she was mute witness to his death. She was about to run for the aluminum canoe banked up on the shore when she saw his dark head break through the waves. Exactly as she had the last time she'd been reassured of his safety, her knees went weak and she sank down on the wet sand. She closed her eyes and rested her clammy forehead on the rock until her stomach stopped jumping.

Eventually she peeped out again, grimacing in silent accusation as she watched him torpedo effortlessly through the water, gliding toward the swimmers' raft that floated farther out in the cove. With his wet brown hair and glistening tanned skin, he reminded her of a sleek sea otter. That animal preferred to cavort in the icy waters of the North Pacific Ocean, and apparently her trespasser didn't mind the cold either.

The longer she watched him, the more entranced she became. The fluid motion of his long body as it cut through the waves was a joy to behold. He was beautiful and as much a part of the natural setting as the gulls that skimmed the gentle, blue swells or the fish that jumped up in the shallows of the cove in search of their morning meal. Swimming past a thicket of water lilies, he playfully slapped the water, startling a pair of loons into full flight.

He laughed in unbridled delight, then floated on his back until the disturbed waterfowl had scolded him with shrill hooting voices and flown out of sight. Jackknifing his legs, he dived deep, giving Chandra a few anxious moments before his shiny dark head finally came back up next to the raft.

She knew that if he climbed up on the float she was going to be given a full frontal display of a magnificently proportioned male body, and dynamite couldn't have budged her from the spot. As soon as she decided that she wouldn't be able to resist seeing his full glory, she also knew that she wasn't going to interrupt his early-morning communion with nature. Tomorrow. Tomorrow if he rode that noisy motorcycle onto her property at sunrise, she'd give him a list of his transgressions, then send him packing. But today. . .doing that to him today would seem almost like sacrilege. Let him think that he had the wilderness lake all to himself, that the only ones sharing his idyll were the graceful cranes fishing by the shore and the curious chipmunks and squirrels that chattered in the fanlike branches of tamarack and spruce that hung out over the water.

Chandra held her breath, trying to withstand the

overwhelming surge of pure sensual awareness that trembled through her body as the man hoisted himself onto the raft and stood up. The pale morning sun highlighted every detail of his strong, muscle-roped limbs and magnificent torso. Shades of gold glinted off the lighter streaks in his hair and shone down on his broad forehead, straight nose and proud jaw. He stood motionless, legs apart, arms braced on slim hips.

Chandra gulped as her gaze fastened on the part of him that proclaimed his manhood, then quickly shifted back up to his face. He looked like a sun god of the Incan civilization, some precious, ancient Indian idol. His smooth flesh and sculpted features radiated an eternal perfection, a timeless virility and an ageless strength.

Chandra could do nothing but stare with worshipful eyes. Sun-sparkled water, like slender strands of wet diamonds, flowed down his body and gathered in a glistening pool at his feet. It came as a shock when the idol moved, raising his arms to prepare for his dive. The sight of him swimming back toward shore, his powerful strokes propelling him swiftly through the clear blue water, finally forced her to move. He couldn't find her gaping at him like an adoring idiot. She had to get out of sight before he gained the beach.

Once again, the boat house served as a screen and she quickly slipped inside. After her eyes had become accustomed to the darkness, she gingerly climbed over the rusty, metal rails of an empty boat lift to reach the small window. Brushing away the cobwebs, she looked out the foggy cracked glass, her eyes trained on the dock.

A full fifteen minutes later, Chandra decided that watching more than six feet of sopping-wet masculinity attempt to dress itself in tight leather clothing was fascinating, often hilarious and vastly entertaining. She had wondered how the more delicate portions of his anatomy could have withstood that jolting landing on the beach, but her concerns were dispelled as soon as he'd pulled two wide elastic straps over his thighs, then adjusted the metal cup he used for protection. Aware that she was behaving no better than a common Peeping Tom, she still hadn't been able to pull her eyes away.

The man's vocabulary had reached a new low as he'd struggled to pull up the second side zipper on his tight pants and had pinched a portion of hair-roughened skin. The brief expletive he'd uttered had been violent and profane. Chandra hadn't been able to stifle her soft laugh but when his head shot up, blazing blue eyes staring toward the boat house, she'd managed to duck quickly away from the window and out of sight.

She hadn't dared to take up her position again until she heard the explosive roar of the motorcycle. Her last glimpse of the man left an indelible impression. Like a ferocious black stallion, the motorcycle reared up on its hind wheel. The dark-clad rider controlled the speeding bike with expertise then, pushing on the handlebars and bringing it back down on both wheels. Bike and rider swerved dangerously close to a stand of young pines, then did a tight turn and charged down the beach.

Chandra listened until the droning of the engine faded in the distance, then let herself out of the boat house. Wanting to see what he had drawn in the sand, she walked across the beach. The waves had washed away part of the writing but she could still make out the words, "Hare and Hounds." She had no idea what they might mean and that only served to increase her curiosity. Who was he and where had he come from? What did he do when he wasn't riding his motorcycle into the ground or skinny-dipping in a secluded lake?

She climbed back up the stairs to the cabin but didn't immediately go inside. She stood on the deck for a long time, not only to savor the sharp tang of pine that permeated the crisp morning air but to replay the past hour in her mind. No man had ever had such a strong effect on her and she hadn't even spoken to him. Yet she felt as if she knew more about him than she'd known about men whom she'd dated for months.

The man flirted with danger, had a reckless streak a mile wide. But he also had a unique love of life and the world in which he lived that struck a responsive chord in her. His daredevil attitude attracted her very much. And she thought that if she ever did meet him, she'd discover he had a highly developed sense of humor. She had seen the sparkle in his eyes and heard his infectious laughter. Although it wasn't obvious, she also sensed a certain vulnerability in him, a sensitivity belied by his macho feats on the motorcycle.

Beyond that, the man had an absolutely gorgeous body. Not one ounce of his flesh went to waste but rather enhanced the whole. Never had she experienced such an intense yearning to touch another

human being, such an instantaneous desire. If her
best friend and business partner, Karen Taylor, knew
of the feelings she'd just had about a perfect stranger
she'd be delighted. Karen felt Chandra had stored
away all of her female urges as soon as the two of
them had formed the partnership of Collins and Taylor, an independent auditing firm.

It was true that Chandra's social life had been
placed on a back burner for over three years, but she
was still young. Thirty wasn't that old, she kept telling herself, even as she felt her biological clock tick-
ing away. She had forced herself not to think about
marriage and children until she had achieved all the
career goals she'd set for herself. After all, Karen was
close to forty, and although she constantly ha-
rangued Chandra about her lack of a love life, she
seemed perfectly content to be single. Oddly, a man
Chandra didn't know and might never see again had
stirred those long dormant, romantic feelings into the
forefront of her thoughts.

After a last wistful look out over the brilliant blue
waters of the lake, Chandra breathed a deep sigh and
stepped back into the cabin. She glanced at the wall
clock that hung over the kitchen sink. It was only six
o'clock! She had a whole day in front of her and
nothing to do. She was no longer the least bit sleepy,
so there was no point in returning to bed. Breakfast,
she decided, astonished by her ravenous hunger.

Her appetite had been practically nonexistent lately. Karen often had to remind her to eat, saying that
one hundred and ten pounds was not enough for a
woman who was five feet four inches tall. Evidently,
the man on the motorcycle had aroused more than

her libido. Indeed, a feeling of exhilaration was singing in her veins.

As soon as she'd eaten, she was going to put on her swimsuit and plunge into the cold water of Willow Lake. She refused to admit that she wanted to do so because she envied and wanted to emulate the free-spirited male who had so recently cavorted in that water.

"I don't get enough exercise," she said aloud, pulling open the refrigerator and removing a carton of eggs and a package of bacon. "I'm going to return to the city in a month, physically fit, minus the office pallor and in a brand-new frame of mind."

She spent the day reliving her childhood, doing all the things she used to do during those halcyon summer vacations—swimming, building sand castles and collecting shells. She climbed the tall hill behind the cabin and ate a picnic lunch on the flat ridge that overlooked the lake. In the late afternoon, she dug up a few worms, then took a bamboo pole and sat on the end of the dock, dangling her bare feet in the water as she fished for her supper.

Chandra's parents had died in a car accident the summer she'd turned fourteen but every year before that they'd spent part of each summer at Willow Lake. Every other year, they'd taken a camping trip to the Rocky Mountains. On weekends they'd gone rock climbing, and in the winter they'd skied. She hadn't wanted to think about those days in fifteen years but now she remembered how much she had loved the physical activity, loved being in the great outdoors during all seasons.

Up until the past three days, she'd rarely taken a

break from work, and though she'd often thought of coming back to Minnesota to the cabin, she hadn't done it. She'd not been sure she was ready to face all the memories. Her life ran on a strict schedule with very little time left over for entertainment or vacations. Her days were spent in long-drawn-out meetings, stuffy offices, her nights in lonely hotel rooms.

She supposed it was inevitable that some of the structured life-style imposed on her by her well-meaning Aunt Rachel and Uncle Harry had rubbed off. They had both been nearly sixty when she'd gone to live with them in Chicago and they hadn't quite known what to do with a precocious teenager. She suspected they had scheduled all those ballet and piano lessons, summer classes in art and foreign languages, to keep her so busy she wouldn't realize how hard it was for them to deal with her. But even if that had been the case, she still loved them dearly.

If it hadn't been for her Aunt Rachel who, even though she'd been supported by her husband for more than forty years, firmly believed that a woman should be self-supporting, Chandra wouldn't have had the money she'd needed to go on to college. Her parents had left her a small trust fund but that had run out before she'd finished high school. The cabin in Arrowhead was the only thing of value left to her and even though selling it would have given her the necessary funds, she couldn't bear to part with it and the wonderful memories of her parents it inspired.

She never would have asked her aunt and uncle for money and had qualified for a partial scholarship to Northwestern, but Aunt Rachel had refused to allow her to get a part-time job at a time when "nothing should interfere with your studies." Uncle Harry had felt Chandra should marry young and had spent a good deal of energy bringing what he thought were eligible suitors to the house. If not for her aunt, she'd probably be celebrating her tenth wedding anniversary with a stuffy banker type.

Instead, Aunt Rachel had persuaded Uncle Harry to finance Chandra's five years of college. She had graduated with a bachelor's degree in accounting and gone on for a master's in business administration. She'd spent the next two years trying to prove to her irascible, elderly uncle that a woman could be every bit as successful in business as a man.

She had exceeded even her own expectations and had been able to pay back every cent her uncle had spent on her education. He hadn't wanted to take the money but he'd seen that, to her, it was a matter of personal pride. Four years ago, she'd gone to work for Karen Taylor and the next year had been offered a full partnership. Collins and Taylor was now a thriving accounting firm, held in high regard by the business world.

It was only lately that Chandra had begun to think about the things she had missed out on by channeling all her energy in one direction. She had plenty of money but no time to spend it, and her few close friends were somehow connected with her business. If she wanted to be perfectly honest, her personal life would rate a zero percentage on a balance sheet and her business life a whopping one hundred.

Unlike her handsome trespasser, Chandra hadn't stopped to smell the roses in years. After making a thorough inventory of her life, she decided a few changes were definitely in order. She might spend her days confined to an office in the city of Duluth working the audit for Hammond Paper Products, but evenings and weekends were her own and she was staying in the perfect setting for some carefree fun in the great outdoors.

That night she fell into bed feeling pleasantly exhausted, and despite a painful sunburn and a scraped knee, she felt wonderful. The last thing she did before falling asleep was to set her alarm for 5:00 A.M.

2

ON MONDAY MORNING, a few minutes before nine o'clock, Chandra walked into the corporate offices of Hammond Paper Products. She'd been up since five and, since the man on the motorcycle had never arrived, she'd had plenty of extra time to get ready for her first meeting with Thaddeus Hammond, the company's president. She had chosen to dress conservatively in a navy linen suit and ivory-colored blouse, hoping her understated clothes would offset the unmanageable riot of sable curls on her head that made her appear much younger than she was.

A few years back, she'd had the natural curls shorn down practically to her scalp but that had just made her look like a fuzzy-headed moppet. Ever since, she'd worn her hair longer but she still had to contend with all the curls and loose tendrils. Any increase in humidity and her hair was a lost cause. Still, except for the gypsylike hair and the small rosebud mouth she'd inherited from her mother, she looked very businesslike and Chandra didn't think it would take much time to convince Mr. Hammond that he'd made the right choice for the job.

The president's secretary ushered her into his office at one minute past nine and Chandra was glad she'd arrived on time. The man liked promptness. Chandra tucked that piece of information away for future reference. Hammond Paper Products was a multimillion-dollar company, her largest client thus far. Chandra intended to make sure the accounting firm of Collins and Taylor would be called upon whenever Hammond needed an outside auditor.

"Mr. Hammond, it's a pleasure to meet you," Chandra offered, extending her hand to the stout, silver-haired man who walked out from behind a large mahogany desk to greet her.

"Ms Collins." Hammond smiled, deepening the crinkled laugh lines around his wide-set gray eyes. His handshake was firm, conveying warmth and confidence. "I appreciate your promptness. The other company officers are waiting for us in the conference room. Let's get the introductions out of the way, then we can get right down to business."

"By all means," Chandra agreed, and made another mental note. Thaddeus Hammond liked efficiency in himself and others.

He opened a side door and waited for Chandra to step in front of him as they proceeded down a long, carpeted hall. "This is the back alley of executive row," Hammond supplied, a chuckle vibrating in his chest. "Until we added on this hall, every time I'd pay a visit to one of my vice-presidents, the rest of my employees would waste time speculating over what was going on." He pointed to an exit door. "My VPs use it to duck out on my visits."

Chandra laughed, relieved to find that he had a sense of humor. "I'll keep this route in mind if I ever need to make a quick getaway."

"Do that," he agreed. "I've found it an invaluable

outlet when my own frustrations get out of hand. Of course, if everyone took advantage of it, we'd have a mass of people milling around all day in the parking lot."

At the end of the hall, Hammond opened a massive door and led Chandra into a large well-lit room, paneled in a lustrous dark wood. A long conference table took up most of the space but the high-backed chairs were vacant, their male occupants forming a single line near the door. Chandra felt as if she was at a formal reception, about to proceed down a receiving line, as she was introduced to the first man who stood waiting to meet her.

Instantly, Chandra switched on the tape recorder in her brain so she'd be able to play back all the names she was learning and recall a few tidbits about each man. Over the next month she'd be working with every one of them, and anything she could learn about their individual personalities would make her job that much easier.

Bob Timmons: vice-president of marketing, surprisingly young, bright red hair, winning smile, boyish charm. "Sales is my game."

Randolph Turner: vice-president of design, roaming eyes, fake smile, flashy dresser. "Randy to a lovely woman like you."

George White: vice-president of operations, suspicious of career women, kindly blue eyes. "Old enough to be your grandfather."

William Baker: vice-president of installation, no distinguishing marks, no distinguishing personality.

Chandra was still trying to come up with a way to remember the forgettable man when Mr. Hammond began introducing her to the last of the line, a tall man in an ill-fitting and noticeably rumpled green suit. "Meet Lincoln Young. Head of finance. We've set you up in his office since he'll have the answers to most of your questions."

"Mr. Young." Chandra lifted her head but the polite smile she had prepared to offer got lost on the way to her mouth. The hand she brought up for the required handshake went limp and dropped back to her side as her astonished eyes riveted through his black horn-rimmed glasses to the bluer-than-blue orbs of the man she'd last seen riding down her beach on a huge, black motorcycle.

A slight furrow developed between his brows and he lowered his own hand since there was no longer anything available for it to shake. His tone was cautious as he replied to her greeting. "Welcome to our company, Ms Collins."

At her continued silence and the intense probing of her dark eyes, he nervously pushed his glasses up on the bridge of his nose. "Eh. . .please feel free to ask me for anything you need. We're fellow accountants and I'm at your service."

Oblivious to the impression she was making, Chandra went on staring, striving to make the connection between the gorgeous naked specimen of virility she had watched dive into her lake and this owlish-looking vice-president of finance. Unconsciously, her bemused brown eyes dropped from the untidy part in his brown hair to the missing button on his slightly wrinkled shirt, then slowly down the unpressed creases of his pants to the scuffed toes of his brown loafers. It couldn't be possible that this disheveled, bookish man was the reckless daredevil who had all but ruined her vacation. It just couldn't be, but it was. She'd have recognized those incredibly blue eyes anywhere.

She didn't realize what she was doing and how it must look until she heard one of the other men conspicuously clear his throat and the subject of her blatant scrutiny began shuffling his feet on the thick brown pile of the carpet. *Oh no*, Chandra thought with dismay. *I've just given him a thorough going-over. What must he be thinking?*

Attempting to cover the lapse, Chandra stated, "Sorry. Just for a minute I thought we'd met before, but I guess not. I'm looking forward to working with you, Mr. Young, and I appreciate your offer of assistance." Making up for what he must have considered a rude slight, she belatedly offered her hand.

She didn't know which one of them was the more embarrassed as their fingers made brief contact, but at least she didn't blush. Lincoln Young wasn't as lucky. A pink tinge crept above the limp collar of his shirt as they both heard Randolph Turner's whispered comment. "Now what's ol' Linc got that I haven't?"

"Gentlemen, take your seats," Thaddeus Hammond instructed as he took Chandra's elbow and steered her to the first chair on the right side of the table. He then took up his own position at the head and promptly launched into the planned agenda.

Unfortunately, Lincoln Young's place was directly across from Chandra's and no matter how hard she tried, she couldn't help stealing glances at him. An accountant! Just like her, though he'd taken a different route and was now a vice-president of a major company.

His present image certainly didn't fit with what she already knew of him. Most accountants she knew were cautious people with analytical minds, logical types who thought long and hard before making decisions. This man had jumped over a lake with absolutely no thought at all, taking a completely illogical risk with his body.

Accountants were fastidious people who appreciated order, but Lincoln Young failed there too. His streaky brown hair was thick and recently washed but looked as if he'd combed it with an eggbeater. And no one would call him well groomed. His shirt had never been introduced to an iron. She was certain the brown tie he was wearing had been purchased a decade before and the suit not long after that. She was fascinated.

As the company president explained the procedures that were to be followed in order to assist Chandra with the annual audit, she began a close study of Lincoln Young's hands, which were toying absently with a pencil. His fingers were long, the nails trimmed short. She was hoping to spot a little engine grease under his nails, physical evidence that he was indeed her early-morning trespasser, but they were scrupulously clean.

The light sprinkle of golden-brown hair on the tops of his hands and above each knuckle was a full shade lighter than that on his head but matched the triangular patch she knew grew on his chest. She could hardly call that unqualified proof of his identity. Still, she knew that these were the same strong, cap-

able hands that she had seen gripping the handlebars
of a powerful bike, expertly controlling its speed. She
wondered how they'd feel against her skin, stroking
her body. Could they be tender hands?

She blinked in surprise when the pencil he was
holding snapped, the pieces flying off in opposite di-
rections. There was an awkward pause in the president's speech as all eyes watched the fragmented
pieces of wood roll slowly across the table's polished
surface and fall off onto the floor.

"Sorry, Thad," Lincoln apologized gruffly, sliding
both hands under the table.

Upon hearing the muffled chuckles and low mut-
terings from those seated farther down, Chandra
realized that, once again, her curious inspection of
Lincoln Young had made him the subject of the
others' amusement. Trying to appear innocent, she
issued a sympathetic smile, praying it would look as
though the broken pencil was the only thing that had
disrupted their meeting.

It was past time she showed that she had a greater
interest in the business at hand than the hands of Lincoln Young. "May I say a few words, Mr. Hammond?"

"Of course," he replied, the glower he aimed at his
chief executives bringing about an immediate calm.

"Since your organization is so large, the only way I
can do a thorough, accurate job is with the coopera-
tion of each department head. Besides the financial
records, I will have to review all contract documents,
agreements with vendors, bond indentures and so
forth. I'll be studying your systems of internal checks
and controls and will interview each one of you to

verify my data. Along with that I'll supervise the physical inventory of the plant."

She lifted her clutch briefcase onto the table and pulled out a stack of management questionnaires. "I would like these returned to me at your earliest convenience. Friday at the latest, please."

Receiving a nod from Hammond, she got up from her chair to pass out the lengthy surveys, stifling a laugh as a series of groans rose up around the table. When she reached Lincoln Young, she made a point of not really looking at him. She merely handed him his copy, then returned to her seat. "Before the name of my firm goes on your annual report, I need answers to each one of the questions on the form I've just handed out. I must be completely satisfied with the accuracy of your statements, or I will have to qualify my opinion on the report."

"And that won't happen, gentlemen," Hammond immediately cut in. "We've had several record months in a row, mainly due to your hard work. I want our stockholders to have absolute confidence in management as we begin the next fiscal year."

The meeting was adjourned half an hour later. As one, the men stood up and pushed in their chairs. Thaddeus Hammond verbally handed her off to Lincoln Young, who didn't look too pleased by the prospect of her company, then proceeded out the door and back down the hall to his private office. The other executives congregated at the end of the table, making small talk, and Chandra sensed they were all waiting to see if her interest in their fellow officer had abated.

She was going to make sure that everyone would

think it had, even though she was more intrigued by the man than ever. After the uncomfortable incident with the pencil, Lincoln Young had done his best to outwardly ignore her and insult her at the same time. On occasion she'd caught him looking at her face, an obvious lack of interest in his expression, and once or twice he'd deliberately looked right through her as if she wasn't there. Because she was aware of him with every nerve in her body, she didn't like the feeling that she left him cold.

Nevertheless, for the next month they'd be sharing an office and, if nothing else, she was going to satisfy her curiosity about him. A good accountant never accepted things at face value and there was far more to Lincoln Young than met the eye. She already knew what kind of quality was hidden by his baggy green suit, but what occupied the space behind his glasses besides a pair of beautiful blue eyes remained a mystery.

"How about meeting me for lunch later?" Randolph Turner suggested as Chandra pushed in her chair and gathered up her papers. "There's a nice restaurant about a mile or so up the highway from here. Believe me, it will beat anything you can buy in the employee cafeteria."

"I appreciate the offer, Mr. Turner," Chandra said tactfully, patting the briefcase tucked under her arm, "but I always brown-bag it for the first few days on a new assignment."

"Randy," he corrected, as his gray eyes traveled over her body. "If you always eat lunch in your office the only one of us who'll have the pleasure of viewing your pretty face will be Linc, and trust me—" he lowered his voice and declared pointedly "—he won't notice."

The man wasn't suggesting that Lincoln Young was gay, was he? That possibility hadn't occurred to her. Then she was jolted by an equally unpalatable thought. What if Lincoln Young was married? Even if he didn't wear a wedding ring he could still be married. No. What kind of wife would let her husband go to work as if he'd slept in his clothes?

Several kinds, Chandra answered her own question. He might be married to a woman who was too busy to worry about the state of her husband's wardrobe. Maybe they had so many children to support he couldn't buy a decent suit. But then how could he afford that expensive motorcycle?

Knowing she was digressing, she conjured up a bright smile and forced herself to address the man she was with. "I appreciate the compliment, Randy. However, until I get a firm handle on the magnitude of an audit, I always hole up in my office with a sandwich. Sorry, but that's Collins policy."

"Then how about dinner tonight? Trust me, you'll find me much more pleasant company than Linc. That guy is all business and you won't get to square one."

Chandra hid her wince and took a quick glance at the others. Did all of them suspect she had set her sights on Lincoln Young? Did they assume she picked out a man on each new assignment and attempted to lure him into her bed? It was obvious that Randolph Turner thought so.

"We could go to my place. I've got a sensational view of Lake Superior from my patio," he promised.

"My special treat for those big brown eyes of yours."

It was far too soon to offend one of the VPs, even if he deserved it, so Chandra simply smiled and kept on walking. Randolph Turner might not be her type but he'd given her reason to think that Lincoln Young was unattached, and that made her unreasonably happy. In an amazingly pleasant tone, she conveyed the stance she always took with overly friendly executives. "According to the C.P.A.'s code of professional ethics I must remain an impartial outsider. I don't get involved with my clients, Randy, and I keep my big brown eyes glued to the books."

"Not so's you'd notice," Turner returned meaningfully.

Chandra bristled and threw his favorite phrase back at him. "Trust me. I do."

At the end of the long table, Lincoln Young stood waiting, far from patiently. In the time it took for her to complete the distance to his side, he'd glanced at his watch twice. One foot tapped noiselessly on the thick carpet.

Randolph Turner gave him an unduly rough pat on the shoulder as he passed by on his way out the door. After catching up with the other men who were ambling slowly down the hallway, Turner called back over his shoulder, "You're a lucky man, Linc ol' buddy. Our lovely auditor says she plans to hole up inside your office. If the rest of us want to see her, we'll have to form a line outside your door."

"Mr. Turner comes on a bit strong," Chandra stated evenly, trying not to show how nettled she was by the man's insinuating comments.

"Randy's all talk, Ms Collins. If you don't en-

courage him, he'll back off." Lincoln dismissed the
incident with a flick of his wrist but behind the
glasses his eyes sent the unmistakable message that
she'd been asking for whatever she got. "I'll show
you where we . . . you'll be working."

Chandra noticed that he was painstakingly careful
not to touch her as they went through the boardroom
door and she was certain he'd have been more comfortable walking three paces behind her as they proceeded down the hall. His was the last office on the
left, and he practically bolted to one side so she
wouldn't brush against him as she entered.

"I don't bite," she snapped irritably, even more annoyed when she saw the doubtful look on his face.
"Listen, Mr. Young. I'm sorry if I've given you the
wrong impression. You really do look just like someone I've seen before. I apologize for being rude."

She had no intention of telling him that that person
was indeed himself, nor that her behavior was the
result of seeing him in all his naked glory. She was
sure he'd be mortified, never wanting to look her in
the face again, and they'd still have to work together.
She couldn't imagine trying to complete her audit
with him turning nine shades of red every time she
spoke to him. On the other hand, it irked her no end
that he obviously didn't find her the least bit attractive. Underneath that sad excuse for a suit he was an
Adonis, but she had a few nice curves herself.

"You're doing it again," Lincoln accused in a
dangerous tone that sounded much more like the
daredevil rider than the mild-mannered accountant.
"Whoever it is I resemble, you obviously feel quite
strongly about him. You're eating me up with your

eyes, Ms Collins. If you don't want to give people the wrong impression, you'd better cut it out."

Guilty as charged, Chandra jerked her gaze toward the farthest corner of the room. "Last time," she assured firmly, schooling her features into a cool mask to hide her total humiliation. "But the resemblance is amazing."

Noticing the clutter on one desk and the clean surface of the other, she walked over to the neat one. Placing her briefcase down on the top, she said, "This one's mine, right?"

"Right," he said. "The first set of books you requested in your letter are stacked on the floor there by the wall." His eyes discouraged further conversation and his next statement confirmed his withdrawal. "Feel free to dig right in. I'm sure you're anxious to get started."

The sooner I get started, the sooner I'll be finished and out of your hair, Chandra thought dryly. She wasn't nearly as anxious to be rid of him as he was of her, she decided with a spurt of self-pity. Life wasn't fair. Here she was sharing an office with Clark Kent, knowing that beneath the disguise was a gorgeous Superman, and he'd have much preferred her to be a hard-nosed Perry White than an adoring Lois Lane. Even worse was the knowledge that the superhero she'd conjured up in her mind was turning out to be a supercilious prig and something of a slob.

"Thanks for preparing a space for me," she muttered ungraciously and sat down on the swivel chair, pretending to test it for comfort and balance. From behind the concealment of her thick lashes, she watched Lincoln take up residence behind his own desk. To her dismay, she found that she would be the only thing that occupied his line of vision. It followed, therefore, that whenever she'd pause in her work, the best view she'd have would be of him. And she kept seeing him minus all of his clothes.

The office was half the size of Thaddeus Hammond's. It had two doors but no windows and although the desks were placed on opposite sides of the room, they faced each other. Having Lincoln in front of her all day long was going to prove very distracting and Chandra would have preferred a different arrangement. From the disturbed look on Lincoln's face, she could tell that he was having the same thought.

Chandra could come up with only one thing that might help her get through the next thirty days. Not stopping to consider how he'd take the question, she blurted in a tone that conveyed great hope, "You wouldn't happen to be gay, would you?"

Lincoln's jaw went slack as his mouth dropped open. Forgetting her promise not to stare, Chandra watched the color run up his cheeks. His Adam's apple bobbed up and down and he choked out, "No, I'm not." Then his jaws clamped tight.

"Too bad." She sighed and made a show of opening the drawers of her desk. She found a box of pencils, several pads of paper, a heavy stapler and all the other office supplies she would need in order to get started. "And you're not married, are you?"

"Not anymore," he confirmed tightly. "I'm divorced."

She didn't dare look at him for several minutes, knowing she'd start to laugh. Chandra Collins made

Lincoln Young extremely nervous and her last remark had really worried him. She supposed it wasn't
very nice of her but since he'd already robbed her of
three good nights of sleep, it was only fair that he suffer something in return.

Feeling his eyes on her, she lifted her long lashes
and pronounced gleefully, "You really shouldn't
stare at me like that, Mr. Young. You're eating me up
with your eyes. Be careful, or you'll give people the
wrong impression."

Chandra then learned that both disdainful accountants and reckless daredevils sputter like teakettles
when tormented. His nostrils flared and his eyes became so brilliantly blue they looked lethal enough to
cut right through her. Ah, revenge was sweet. But so
was her smile.

An angry red flush covered Lincoln's neck and shot
up his cheeks but his tone was calm. "I was expecting
a human calculator, Ms Collins. Forgive me, if I'm a
bit shocked that I'm sharing an office with a . . . ."

Evidently sensing he was about to put a foot in his
mouth, he hastily concluded, "A young woman.
Since you're a full partner in your own firm, I assumed you'd be much older."

He then proceeded to ram both feet all the way
down his throat. "You don't look or act old enough
to be out of high school."

"I'm thirty," she informed him smoothly, looking
down to hide the slow burn that smoldered in her
brown eyes. "I guess that's considered young to be
a full partner in any firm, but it's just a case of
hard work paying off. How did you get to be vice-
president here at . . . what? Thirty-four, thirty-five?"

"Thirty-three. And you're right, hard work does pay off so let's get to it."

"By all means, Mr. Young." She made his name sound like a dirty word.

"Look, I'd feel much more comfortable calling you Chandra," he announced in a reluctant tone.

If that was a bid for a more friendly atmosphere, Chandra thought it was entirely too low, so she remained silent.

"If we're going to be roommates for a whole month, Ms Collins seems a bit formal," he persisted more loudly.

Chandra arched one brow at the word *roommate* and couldn't resist taking one more potshot at him. He'd shot her down enough times. "Roommates, huh? Looks to me like I'm sharing an office with an outrageous flirt, but there shouldn't be any harm in calling each other by our first names. Just don't take it as my permission for even greater intimacies, Lincoln."

"I wasn't . . . dammit . . . I'm not—"

"I know." Chandra giggled, then laughed the infectious musical laugh that she hadn't uttered for years and years. "But it's such fun to tease you, Lincoln Young. Don't let this go to your head, but your blush is really cute—an unexpected pleasure in a man. I'll bet women say all sorts of indecent things to you just to inspire that marvelous color that comes up in your face."

"Excuse me." Lincoln shoved back his chair and stood up. The face in question was a deep shade of rose but cute wasn't the word to describe it. Outraged dignity sparkled in his eyes as he strode to the door that led to the back hallway. "I've got a meeting to attend. I don't know when I'll be back."

As soon as you take a few laps around the parking lot and cool off, Chandra thought. But she gave him a jaunty little wave and in her most seductive voice drawled, "Don't worry about me. I've got enough to keep me busy for hours. We can get together later." *After you've located that sense of humor I know you've got hidden somewhere down deep inside you.*

The door didn't exactly slam but it wasn't closed softly either, and Chandra emitted another giggle. So far, meeting up with her trespasser had proved to be somewhat ego-deflating but exhilarating at the same time. She hadn't had this much fun, felt this alive, in years and no matter what else happened the next month wasn't going to be boring.

Lincoln Young was a total enigma to her. He was hot-tempered but exercised a rigid control. He loved the outdoors, yet held down a job that kept him tied to a windowless office. He owned expensive leathers for riding but had spent next to nothing for the green suit he had on. He swam naked with no hint of modesty, then blushed like a kid when a woman made a suggestive comment. In order to ride his motorcycle so proficiently, he had to have keen eyesight, yet as an accountant who spent hours reviewing financial data, he evidently needed glasses.

There was nothing she relished more than ferreting out the underlying reasons for something that varied from the norm. Usually the problems she dealt with related to figures but she wasn't averse to working out a human puzzle. Lincoln Young intrigued her far more than any man ever had. She couldn't wait for him to return so she could begin fitting all the pieces together, discovering the whole picture of the man.

3

"SHE'S A DAMNED BARRACUDA!" Linc announced to the rear bumper of his Chevy pickup truck as he stalked past the first line of vehicles parked in the employee lot. Angrily, he pulled off his glasses and slipped them into his coat pocket.

His face wore a fierce scowl as he acknowledged that his low estimation of Chandra Collins's personality did nothing to allay the acute tension she'd caused in his body. Jamming both hands into the pockets of his trousers, he fought back the tidal wave of sexual responses that had been washing over him ever since he'd been introduced to the woman. It was almost an hour later and he could still feel her sultry dark eyes stripping off his clothes and taking slow measure of his physique.

Not since his days on the racing circuit had a woman issued that obvious an invitation and he'd almost forgotten what it felt like. At first, the adulation of the female groupies who'd trailed after the bikers had surprised and flattered him, but eventually he'd got used to the attention and learned to ignore it. Today's episode had been so unexpected, he'd behaved like an out-and-out fool.

Every man at the table had been able to see the sensual expression on Chandra's face as she'd devoured him with her eyes, but he should have had enough control not to react like a nervous virgin. He might have gone a long time without a woman, but that was still no excuse for his juvenile reaction to her.

Recalling the embarrassing incident with the broken pencil, Linc swore out loud. He was sure she considered him a small-town hick, and if her behavior in the office was any indication she planned to continue her flirtatious antics just to watch him squirm. What had she called his furious blush? An unexpected pleasure in a man? Hell! He hadn't gone red like that since he'd worked up his courage and kissed Sue Ellen Forbes in the fifth grade.

Chandra Collins. He mulled the name over and over again in his mind. Where had he heard that name before?

Usually his excellent memory provided him with instant recall, but even though he knew he'd heard of her, he couldn't remember where or when. He did know it had nothing to do with her work. Her signature on the recent correspondence exchanged between her firm and Hammond Paper hadn't struck a chord with him either.

Then why did he have the impression that she really did know him from somewhere? He had sensed that she was secretly laughing at him when she'd made that flimsy excuse about his resembling someone else. That line was as old as the hills and did little to explain her continued provocative behavior in his office.

Once they were alone, she had turned the tables on him, teased him for becoming too personal, when only minutes before she'd acted as if she desired the most personal kind of relationship there was. It was incredible. She was incredible.

"How could I forget meeting a woman like her?" he muttered, a perplexed furrow between his brows.

Chandra Collins was far too attractive a woman to forget. She was downright beautiful in his estimation. Before he'd discovered how treacherous members of her sex could be, her striking looks would have drawn him to her like a magnet. She gave her age as thirty, but her flawless complexion, soft willful mouth and that wild mass of dark glossy hair made her look like a teenage siren.

Even the ultraconservative suit she wore couldn't hide the fact that she had all the right curves in all the right places. When she'd stood up and begun flirting with Randolph Turner, it was all he could do to keep his eyes off the silky contours of her surprisingly long legs and the way her tight derriere thrust against the straight line of her skirt.

If truth were told, the only thing he didn't like about her was that blatant come-hither act of hers. He'd been chased one too many times and knew the kind of disaster that could come with being caught. He wouldn't allow that to happen to him again, not even with a woman who looked like Chandra.

If and when he ever became involved with another woman it wouldn't be with a sophisticated, city type like her, who'd probably die if she ever got dirt under her perfectly manicured nails. He'd stay away from her even if she did affect him more strongly than any woman he'd met in years. He'd felt the same kind of sexual pull with Jean, and all he had to show for his five years of marriage to her was the huge dent in his bank balance from the divorce settlement. Jean had kept the house, the furniture, the new car—everything.

In order to send his three boys on to college, he was going to have to work his tail off for several more years to make up the deficit Jean had caused in his finances. Because of the boys, he didn't have time to cultivate meaningful relationships and couldn't afford to think with his hormones instead of his brain. Jean had taught him just how much that could cost. It had been a hard lesson but it was one he'd never forget.

What was wrong with him today? It might have been a while but he knew how to deal with an overly aggressive woman. Chandra Collins was in for a big surprise if she continued playing games with him. He might not be as immune to her pretty face and curvaceous body as he would have liked, but a woman who threw herself at a man she barely knew wasn't worth the price of a good beer.

CHANDRA WASN'T USUALLY A CLOCK-WATCHER and she had never put in such a long and uncomfortable afternoon. She couldn't wait to get out of Lincoln Young's office. He'd returned after lunch but instead of taking up where they'd left off, he'd totally shut her out. Behind his glasses his eyes had been like twin glaciers, and Chandra realized that his escape into the parking lot had increased his bad temper, rather than the reverse.

By the end of the day they hadn't exchanged more than a few sentences, and then only because Chandra had needed his help to find some additional ledgers that weren't included in the pile near her desk. His terse comments had conveyed all the warmth of ice water. She was more than put out by his deliberate silence and was as anxious as he to vacate their shared premises.

"I'm leaving now," she said the instant she heard the five o'clock whistle coming from the plant.

Lincoln lifted his head long enough to give her a curt nod, then immediately lowered his eyes back to the computer printout he'd been studying for the past two hours.

Thoroughly vexed by his rudeness, Chandra remarked coldly, "Aren't you being somewhat childish over this? I was only teasing this morning. If I'd known you have no sense of humor, I wouldn't have given you such a hard time."

For the first time in hours, he established eye contact with her. "What are you talking about, Chandra? How am I being childish?"

"By refusing to talk to me all day long and by making me feel like a leper," she retorted, even though she felt foolish admitting that his behavior had really got under her skin.

She could have sworn he was holding back laughter, except that his eyes remained cold. His tone was calm as he replied to her charge, so calm she felt like even more of a fool. "As an accountant, you should know that working with numbers often requires total concentration. I'm sorry if you feel I was deliberately ignoring you."

One brow rose as he gave her a considering look. "Do you normally waste time on meaningless chit-chat with your clients when conducting an audit of their finances?"

The man had gone past his dismissal of her womanly charms and was attacking her professional abilities! Chandra wouldn't stand for it. Gritting her teeth, she countered, "When conducting an audit, I normally try to establish some kind of rapport with my co-workers. It's time-consuming and sometimes very difficult to gather all the specific data I need, so it helps to have a good working relationship with the financial officer."

Again he lapsed into silence but this time Chandra didn't feel as if he were shutting her out. This time it appeared more likely that he was simply mulling something over in his mind. Even though he'd been acting like a total jerk all afternoon, she still longed to reach out and massage away the lines of tension on his forehead, the tightness around his mouth. She'd seen his face when he was totally relaxed and he'd been twice as handsome then. She didn't like to think that she was the cause of his strained expression.

"Perhaps we should start over at dinner, Chandra," he finally offered, taking off his glasses to massage the bridge of his nose. "I would like to explain a few things concerning our system of operations and I'd like to do it before you get too far along.

"I got so involved in my own business today that I've neglected your legitimate need for further explanation. A company's books are seldom self-explanatory, and I'm aware that there are several items in our inventory that must seem like Greek to you."

"Thank you. I do need some translation." Chandra was relieved by his change in attitude, until she realized he might think she was jumping at the chance to go out with him. "It's been a long day. How would it be if we agreed to sit down together and go over a few points first thing in the morning?"

"It would be better for me if we could do it now," he replied, a minuscule thawing evident in his eyes. "We both have to eat tonight and I'll be in meetings all morning. We're negotiating new contracts with our union and you know how that goes."

His logic was indisputable so Chandra gave in. "All right. Do you have a place in mind? I'm unfamiliar with the area; it's been years since I've been here."

"Were you here on vacation?"

Chandra began stuffing papers into her briefcase and wasn't thinking when she answered him. "Sort of. My folks owned a cabin on Willow Lake. It's about forty miles north of here. We'd drive down to Duluth every once in a while but I can't remember any of the restaurants we used to go to."

She picked up her purse and walked around the desk, coming to a startled halt when she found Lincoln staring at her as if she'd suddenly grown another head. "Is something wrong?"

"What?" Linc asked as if he hadn't heard the question, then proved that he had by hastily negating, "No, nothing at all. I was just thinking that it's a small world. That is, if your Willow Lake is the same one I'm thinking of."

And I know damned well it is, Linc swore silently. That's where he'd seen her name before. Henry was the caretaker for her fifty acres of land!

I saw the letter she wrote Henry at the beginning of summer. Think back, he ordered himself. Had she mentioned that she was coming to stay for a while? No, there'd been no hint of that. Not one member of the Collins family had been to the cabin in years. So many years, that he and Henry almost thought of the property surrounding Willow Lake as their own.

"I doubt it, but it's a common name. I know of three others within a hundred-mile radius," Chandra noted nonchalantly. "My cabin is the only one on the lake. It's in a very isolated section of forest, far off the beaten track."

Chandra watched him from beneath the sweep of her lashes, hoping to see some reaction. So far, nothing but open curiosity, she judged and kept her hands busy replacing pencils and papers inside her desk. Not only did she hope to rattle him a little, but she was curious herself and hoped he'd relate how he'd become so familiar with her land.

The lake was rarely shown on state maps and few people would have searched it out using a top map. She doubted if many of the locals knew of its existence, it was so isolated. She could think of only one logical way by which he might have discovered its location. Continuing in the same nonchalant manner, she stated, "Unless you've used an Indian guide named Henry Raincloud, I'd be surprised if you're even aware it exists. He and his family are the only ones who have access to the property. Henry owns some shoreline and I own the rest. He's been my caretaker for years."

"I do know Henry and it's the same Willow Lake," Linc replied with equal nonchalance, but Chandra saw something else register in his eyes.

She had some difficulty keeping a straight face as she inquired, "You've used Henry as a guide?"

The rapid rise and fall of Lincoln's Adam's apple was the only visible sign that her question might have caused him some discomfort. Chandra did notice that he kept his gaze firmly directed at the wall beyond her when he stated, "I went fishing with him on opening day."

Still not looking directly at her, Linc went on casually, "I've seen your cabin. He told me the owners hadn't used it for fifteen years. I bet he was surprised when you showed up."

Chandra put off rearranging pencils in the drawer and looked him straight in the eye. "Maybe so but he had everything ready for me when I got there."

This time there was no mistaking the shock her statement had made. The beginnings of a familiar pink tinge rising up his neck gave him away and Chandra wanted to giggle at the difficulty he was having maintaining his cool. If the man blushed when she stared at his fully clothed body, there was no telling what shade of scarlet he would turn when he discovered she'd studied him nude.

Having great difficulty keeping a straight face, Chandra went in for the kill. "I got in last Thursday night."

She hesitated, gauging his reaction. Instead of turning a deeper shade of red as she'd expected, he'd paled. She wasn't normally given to making others uncomfortable, but for some reason she was taking particular delight in watching this man squirm. Maybe it had something to do with his earlier disdainful attitude toward her and how he'd ignored her all afternoon. Well, he wasn't ignoring her now! His eyes were all but bugging out of his head as he searched her expression and she knew exactly what he was searching for.

Having too much fun letting him dangle in uncertainty, Chandra went blithely on. "I wrote Henry a letter telling him to expect me but he wasn't there to greet me when I arrived. I stopped by his place on the way in but no one was home. There was a note on the door that said he'd taken his grandsons camping for a few days. I'm lucky my letter reached him before he left. Otherwise I wouldn't have had any heat and it really gets cold at night."

Chandra was extremely gratified by Linc's reaction to this confirmation of her arrival date. He appeared to be having trouble digesting her words and repeated them twice, as much to himself as to her. "Last Thursday? Thursday night?"

Linc tried to shift his brain into a higher gear but Chandra's announcement had really jammed up the cogs. *Think! Did you see a car? Smoke coming from the chimney?* No, he hadn't seen anything but that didn't necessarily mean there'd been nobody there. Her car could have been parked in the garage and if the heat had been turned on in the cabin there would have been no reason to have a fire going. "So... then you've been out there for almost four days."

"You add very well," Chandra complimented his comical understatement. "That must be why you took up accounting."

"Maybe so," he mumbled, completely oblivious to the humor of her remark.

Linc gave her another long searching glance but there was nothing in her expression to indicate that she knew about his early-morning rides on his motorcycle. Still, a discomfiting suspicion was growing in his mind. She'd been there and he'd driven very close to the cabin. Only an extremely sound sleeper wouldn't have heard him.

Somehow, Linc didn't believe the bright-eyed woman in front of him would have slept through the grinding roar of a motorcycle engine. She had to have heard him, of that he had no doubt, but beyond that? If she'd seen him on any one of the past three mornings, it would certainly explain her behavior today. What if . . . ? He could feel another flush coming on.

When Henry got back home with the boys he was going to wring the old man's neck for not telling him that Chandra had taken up residence in the cabin. In the meantime, he was going to find out how much she'd seen and do his best to get her out of that cabin. He didn't want her unsettling presence to threaten his boys or the life-style he was leading.

"It must be awfully quiet at the lake compared to what you're used to," Linc asserted as he pulled open a desk drawer and placed his glasses inside.

"Very peaceful," she agreed, biting off the rest of the statement, *except for the early-morning intrusion of a very sexy motorcyclist.* "It's a refreshing change from city life."

"Are you planning to stay way out there the whole time you're at Hammond?"

His hope that her stay had been planned for only the weekend died when she readily answered, "Saves me the price of a hotel."

"Forty miles is quite a long haul to make twice a day," he said in an attempt to discourage her. He didn't tell her that he'd been doing it for the past three years and enjoyed every minute of the scenic drive.

"Wouldn't it be better to get a hotel in town? Take

tonight for instance . . ." Linc persisted as he ushered her into the hall.

Not on your life, Chandra wanted to answer. *I wouldn't want to miss your early-morning skinny-dips. Being a crack-of-dawn voyeur could become habit-forming.* She had to give him credit, he was managing to keep his tone indifferent. "I don't mind the drive."

Digging into his pant pocket, Linc took out his keys to lock up the office. "But if it takes us a few hours to get through our meeting, you'll have to make that drive in the dark. I remember the road that goes in there. It's full of curves and ruts." *Come on, city lady. Admit you're scared silly to be out there in the middle of nowhere!* "You could get in an accident and no one would find you for months."

Chandra was enjoying this conversation immensely. *The plot thickens*, she remarked to herself. Not only was Lincoln unwilling to admit that he'd been on the property at least three times in the past week, he was hoping to persuade her to stay elsewhere. Why? So she wouldn't catch him trespassing, or was there some other reason?

She already knew he was modest but surely there was more to his little campaign to get rid of her than the fear that she might see him skinny-dipping. He could always fess up to the trespassing, ask for her permission and forgo the swim. It was more likely that he was trying to hide something other than his body. Intriguing.

"I appreciate your concern but I'm not worried. I'm a good driver. Besides, it's only five o'clock. We could talk for hours and it would still be light when I got back to my cabin."

Out in the parking lot, Chandra pointed to the car she'd rented at the airport, a pale blue Ford Escort, then said she should follow him to the restaurant so neither of them would have to come back to the lot. With an air of relief, he agreed instantly and took a step toward a dusty pickup truck.

"I wasn't planning to take a lady to dinner so the seats aren't very clean," he admitted, but that didn't stop him from climbing in without considering the possible damage to his suit.

Of course, Chandra thought, that suit couldn't look much worse than it already did. The poor thing needed to be retired, given a decent burial or whatever one did for a favorite suit that was long past its prime. Surely, the financial officer of a firm as large as Hammond Paper could afford to dress a bit more fashionably. Considering the outfit she'd seen him wearing the other day, the miserable green suit seemed more like a purposefully chosen costume than a reflection of his taste.

"I've never met an accountant who drives a truck," Chandra said thoughtfully. "You don't seem the type." *Not the type you show this part of your world, at least.*

But the truck had four-wheel drive and was exactly the kind of thing a biker would need to haul a heavy machine around, especially if he competed in any races. Would a man Lincoln's age race motorcycles? If the performance she'd witnessed yesterday was any indication of his skill, she decided he might not only race but win.

"I've got a place out in the country," Linc explained. "An accountant who's almost completed the process of building a new house drives a truck into town so he can bring back the supplies."

"Oh? Are you building it yourself?" Chandra asked.

"No, but I'm acting as the general contractor to save myself some money. When materials are needed, I'm the one who goes to get them."

He leaned down to switch on the ignition and Chandra took the hint. She walked the short distance to where her car was parked. By the time she had backed out of the spot Thaddeus Hammond had reserved for her use, Lincoln's truck was already at the plant entrance. He waited for her to catch up but then, instead of turning left toward the city, he turned right, heading north out of town.

They drove down the highway for at least five miles before he pulled off onto a dirt road. Where was he taking her, Chandra wondered, surely not to his place? He'd made it clear that this was to be a working meal so he wouldn't take her home with him, would he? Of course she wouldn't mind if he did. She would love to satisfy her curiosity about the kind of place he lived in. He said he was almost finished building a new house. Would it mirror the tastes of the accountant or the dirt biker? She was ready to place her money on the latter.

Chandra soon discovered that she wasn't going to learn the answer to that question on their present outing. Lincoln pulled his truck into a gravel parking lot surrounded by tall stands of red cedar. Chandra parked her car and stared dubiously through the windshield at the square, one-story building in front of her.

The outside walls were white but the paint was

chipping badly and bare wood showed through in several places. Spiderwebs and several wasp nests clung to the eaves and a gray coating of lake flies plastered the windowless exterior. The flat roof was covered with what looked like tar paper. Blue smoke rose from several small pipes that appeared to be makeshift chimneys at the rear of the building.

The parking lot was almost full but there was nothing else to indicate that a restaurant was housed inside the ramshackle structure. And even if there was one, Chandra wasn't too sure she wanted to risk eating in it. She couldn't imagine what Lincoln was trying to prove by taking her to a place like this. Who knows, she thought rather bleakly, perhaps he enjoyed taking risks not only with the exterior of his body but with the interior as well.

When Lincoln pulled open the car door, she caught the flicker of amusement in his eyes before he blinked it away. *That does it*, Chandra declared inwardly. This was some kind of test and she was determined to pass it no matter what they were serving in there.

For some unknown reason she felt that proving herself a good sport to this man would be worth it. Besides, it shouldn't be too difficult. She wasn't a squeamish person and she was a good sport! She might not have done so for a long time but she'd had plenty of experience roughing it.

"Lake Superior is right down there." Linc nodded toward the thick trees. "You can't see it from where we're standing but you can smell it."

Chandra inhaled deeply and sighed with pleasure as the clean fresh tang of the water filtered down into her lungs. "So you can. Before I go back to Chicago,

I'm going to take a drive along Skyline Parkway. You get such a breathtaking view of the lake from up there on the ridge. I used to love making that trip."

At her rapturous expression, Linc couldn't hold back the question that had been bothering him ever since he'd discovered who she was. "If you loved it so much, why haven't you come back until now?"

"In the past few years it was because I was so caught up in my work," Chandra said honestly. "Before that, it was because I couldn't bear to come. I was fourteen when my parents died. It took me a long time to be able to face the wonderful memories I had of the summers we spent up here.

"I couldn't bring myself to part with the cabin but I didn't want to see it. Now I plan to enjoy everything I used to do as a kid. Yesterday I caught three fish and had them for supper. Nothing tastes as good as fresh walleye." She was gratified by the look of astonishment on his face.

Linc couldn't believe what he had just heard. With the exception of her unruly hair, she was the picture of sophistication—expensive clothes, perfect makeup. He couldn't quite make the association between the professional career woman and the woman who would catch her own supper. Maybe she wasn't alone at the cabin. "Who cleaned them for you?"

Chandra grinned and playfully scolded him with a raised finger. "I did of course. I don't know what the rule is in your family but ours was, 'You catch 'em, you clean 'em.'"

Beginning to think they were never going to get out of the parking lot, Chandra gestured toward the building. "Is there really a decent restaurant in there?"

"One of my favorites," Linc affirmed, taking hold of her elbow. "It's run by Racine and Ned White-water. They moved off the reservation and started this place about five years ago." There seemed to be an element of personal pride in his voice as he went on, "It's doing great."

"It is?" Chandra couldn't hide her doubt as they neared the door. She was beginning to wonder if she was up to this test as Lincoln reached for the screen door leading to a porch. Casting a quick glance at her escort she saw that his smile was the most natural one she'd seen on his face all day. Damn! He'd detected her hesitation. Plucking up her courage, she stepped through the doorway and waited, plastering as sincere a look of expectancy on her face as she could.

"Racine makes the best venison stew in the world," he declared.

Chandra tried not to wrinkle her nose but wasn't completely successful. The one time she'd had venison, she'd been about five years old and had had difficulty chewing the stringy, strongly flavored meat. The thought that it might have been one of Bambi's relatives hadn't helped matters either, despite her father's explanations about herd control. As an adult, she understood the reasons hunting was legal and actually necessary to keep the animals from starving in the winter. But as a child no amount of logic had encouraged her to develop a taste for game.

Evidently, Lincoln had been waiting for the slightest sign of distaste for he immediately charged, "If you haven't tried it, don't knock it."

"I've eaten deer meat before and I didn't like it,"

she protested lamely. "Isn't there anything else on the menu?"

"Sure," Linc verified but Chandra spied the gleam of laughter in his eyes.

Reading her expression, he attempted to appease her suspicion. "The Whitewaters are famous around here. Their place might not be very fancy but their food's like nothing you ever tasted."

On the outside, the building looked run-down but the inside was decorated in the traditional manner of clubs along the North Shore. The booths that lined the walls were wide, the seats covered with red vinyl. The Formica tables were edged with chrome. Game trophies were hung all over the knotty-pine paneling. There were at least ten huge mounted fish, the heads of several deer and one moose. A mammoth stuffed bear, its dangerous-looking paws clawing the air, was displayed prominently near the entrance.

What pleased and surprised Chandra was the back wall, which was all windows. Not only did the glass let in the outside light but it provided a panoramic view of Lake Superior. As she and Lincoln seated themselves at one of the tables nearest the windows, Chandra gazed out at the vast body of water. She could make out four iron-ore boats on the horizon. They were so far away that they looked like thin, black cigars floating beneath low-hanging, cotton clouds.

"This is wonderful." Chandra beamed her approval at Lincoln. "It only goes to show that outside appearances are often deceiving." Her comment about the interior was sincere even if she was still having reservations about the food.

Linc nodded, looked as though he was about to say something, then abruptly turned his attention to the view when the waitress produced their menus. Chandra followed his gaze out the window but could see nothing that might have caused the strange look that had come over his features. He also appeared to be having trouble swallowing.

Chandra wondered with a small amount of glee whether he was placing more on her last statement than she'd intended. His reaction might be an indication that he suspected she'd seen him by the lake. Double entendre was not normally one of her fortes but perhaps she'd unwittingly struck home.

As soon as she scanned the list of entrées, Chandra knew why Linc was struggling to maintain a straight face. She hadn't been as inadvertently clever as she'd thought. Almost every item on the menu was made from plants or animals found in the wild. Rabbit, venison, frogs' legs, quail pie—even moose. Chandra was sure she couldn't stomach a buffalo burger. She didn't even recognize some of the side dishes. What on earth was Chippewa bannock? Did people actually eat cattail pollen?

With studied serenity, Chandra placed her elbows on the table and rested her chin on her clasped hands. "So you recommend the venison stew? What about the Crawfish Bake? It's billed as a gourmet's delight."

Linc could no longer contain himself and burst out laughing. "You're a good sport, Chandra. I suppose I should have warned you, but I didn't want to miss the look on your face when you read the menu. You reacted with commendable poise. Some of the people I've brought in here were back out the door before I could convince them they were in for a real treat."

"I don't blame them. That will take some convincing."

In the end, however, it was Chandra who had a hard time persuading Linc to try some of the elderberry flower fritters she'd ordered for dessert. She'd already finished off every morsel of the rich, flavorful stew and had used a portion of bannock, a kind of flat doughy bread, to wipe the last bit of gravy from her plate. Throughout the entire meal, neither one of them had brought up business. They were much too busy savoring the different but marvelous meal and each other's unexpectedly enjoyable company.

"Where's your spirit of adventure, Lincoln?" Chandra challenged, her dark eyes shining like polished ebony as she tried to push a small piece of the golden-brown cake past his stubbornly closed lips.

Linc leaned back out of reach. "I ate a bunch of elderberries when I was a kid and had the worst stomachache of all time."

"Chicken," she teased, but gave up trying to persuade him. "Oh, look!" She gazed out the window. "Isn't that a beautiful sailboat?"

"Beautiful," he acknowledged, but his eyes were on her. His tone was bemused. Chandra didn't notice, which was good because Linc wasn't ready to admit how he felt about her.

He didn't quite know how it had happened, since she definitely was not his type, but he wanted her. This morning her actions had turned him off, but tonight? Tonight he found her charming. So charming that all he could think about was what it would be like to make love to her, to make those enchanting eyes of hers reflect his image and to hear his name cried from her soft lips.

When Chandra looked back at him he wore the expression of a starving man. He promptly lowered his gaze to her plate. "I guess it wouldn't hurt to try one of those berry things. Can't have you thinking I'm a coward."

"Way to go, hotshot!" Chandra enthused, recalling too late where she'd last heard the comment. The color drained from her face but she valiantly went on, hoping he wouldn't think anything of it. After all, when she'd thought she'd accidentally delivered a witty entendre earlier, it hadn't been the case. "Taking a few risks makes life worthwhile, don't you think?"

"Oh, I do," Linc agreed, his eyes watching her trembling fingers as she offered him a piece of her dessert. So she had seen him and now she was afraid to admit it. Interesting, he deemed, considering how she'd tortured him before, letting him wonder how much she'd witnessed. She wasn't as sophisticated as she would have had him believe.

Slowly, holding her gaze with eyes that were suddenly a fathomless shade of blue, he reached for the fritter and brought it to his lips. "Geronimo!" he murmured softly just before he bit into the sugary dough.

4

HE KNEW! Chandra felt a sudden queasiness in her stomach and quickly lowered her gaze but the feeling didn't abate. Without looking at Lincoln, she could still picture his strong white teeth sinking deep into the fritter as his blue eyes penetrated her own. *Good grief! What should I do now?* Chandra stared into her coffee.

The secret knowledge she had of him had amused her all day but it didn't seem nearly as funny now that he was in on the joke. What was she going to say if he confronted her with what she knew? His delectation of the flower fritter had seemed a bit too predatory for comfort and she feared that she would soon be forced to swallow some of the flirtatious remarks she'd made to him today.

Chandra picked up her coffee cup but her fingers were shaking and she jostled some of the hot liquid on her wrist. "Oh!" she cried softly, as she replaced her cup in the saucer and grabbed for a napkin. Glad of any diversion, Chandra dabbed at her wrist even though the stinging sensation had already been effectively doused by the air. Eyes down, she still got the unsettling impression that Lincoln was doing a rapid reevaluation of her in light of what he now knew. What if he challenged the desire he'd seen in her eyes all morning?

"Did you burn yourself?" Linc inquired solicitously, though Chandra sensed a smile lurking behind his lips.

"It's fine," Chandra quickly assured him, trying hard to think of a way to bring their dinner to a very abrupt end.

She was taken aback when Lincoln reached across the table and took hold of her hand. Cradling her palm in his warm fingers, he gently stroked the slightly reddened splotch on her slender wrist. "It doesn't look serious but with your delicate skin it must hurt."

It took all of Chandra's willpower not to snatch her hand out of his grasp. "It's fine," she repeated nervously, sure that he couldn't help but notice the heated flush that was steadily mounting in her cheeks.

"Good," Linc pronounced, but instead of releasing her hand, he dipped a paper napkin into his water glass and applied it to her wrist. "I've always found cold water does a good job bringing down the body temperature."

He smiled, eyes dancing with amusement, as more color rushed to her face. "Now, isn't that better?"

"Much better," Chandra agreed, though with every second that passed her skin felt hotter. When she could stand it no longer, she pulled her hand away. The crude compress fell off her wrist and onto the floor. Wanting any excuse to break the sudden and acute sexual tension between them, she bent over to retrieve the wet napkin.

In the past few seconds, Lincoln had made it clear what he planned to do. Unless she came right out and told him that she'd spied on him, he'd take the offensive and methodically cut away at her with the punishing sword of innuendo. Unfortunately, she didn't have the courage to broach the subject, nor the sophistication to withstand much more of his pointed visual and verbal thrusts.

Straightening, she glanced at her watch and was surprised to see that it was nearly nine o'clock. "Thank you for a very interesting dinner, Lincoln. I—"

"Call me Linc. Everyone does."

Chandra was willing to call him anything if it meant she could hasten her departure. "I really enjoyed this, Linc, but it's getting late. I'd better get going while there's still some light." She stood and picked up her purse. "Stay and enjoy your coffee. I'll see you at the office tomorrow."

"I'll pay the bill and walk out with you," Linc said, as he rose and reached into his coat for his wallet. He placed a generous tip on the table, then took a polite grasp on her elbow. "I'm glad we had dinner together. It certainly cleared up a few misconceptions I've had about you. After tonight, I think we both know each other a bit better and that should make it easier for us to work together. Don't you agree?"

"I suppose so," Chandra replied, sincerely doubting it. His fingers seared through her linen jacket and silk blouse as if they had the power to make the material disintegrate, as if he could feel her bare skin. She tried to control her erratic breathing as he guided her toward the front of the restaurant.

"You sound as if you've got some reservations."

"Not at all," she managed when he released her

elbow in order to pay their bill at the register. She didn't have any reservations whatsoever. She wanted to avoid him completely or at least keep out of his way until she learned more about him. He was still an enigma to her and tonight had only increased her confusion.

Very few of her questions about him had been answered during dinner and several more had arisen. If he wasn't at all introverted, why had he behaved as he had in the office? Was that soft glow in his beautiful eyes for real or was it just his way of making her highly uncomfortable with her too intimate knowledge of his boy?

Chandra garnered enough poise to behave naturally as Linc ushered her outside into the parking lot, but she didn't know how long she could endure. Earlier in the day, he had been the one who had made a point of keeping his distance. Now it was she who had to force herself not to flinch whenever he touched her.

As they made their way toward her car, he walked uncomfortably close beside her. She was positive the occasional brush of his arm against her side was deliberate and meant to entice her. It was going to be a very long month. "Good night," she stated much too emphatically as she unlocked her car and slid behind the wheel. "And thanks again for dinner," she tacked on hastily, turning the key in the ignition.

"The pleasure was all mine, Chandra." His voice was a low, seductive drawl, full of deeper meaning. "I'll look forward to seeing you in the office tomorrow. It's going to be an enjoyable month."

"That's a matter of opinion," Chandra said aloud

as soon as she had backed out of her parking space and was heading for the exit. She glanced in her rearview mirror and saw Linc staring after her, his face split in a broad grin. She groaned, then stepped on the gas and sped away. She had ignored her first instincts and misjudged him completely! Underneath the facade of a reserved accountant, he was reckless and daring—definitely the aggressive man she'd seen on that gleaming black motorcycle.

It was growing dark when she reached the cutoff to her cabin. She made the turn, then checked her rearview mirror, her temper rising when she saw the headlights of the pickup. He was following her! At first, when she'd spotted his truck, she had thought his route home was similar to her own and that he'd eventually turn off, but now she knew that wasn't the case. Besides Henry Raincloud's, there was only one other cabin on this road—hers.

Although she'd hoped to postpone facing the consequences of her behavior at his office, Chandra realized that the showdown was imminent. But there was no way she was going to allow him to follow her all the way home. She winced as she recalled the provocative lilt that had been in her voice earlier in the day as she'd pronounced, "We can get together later."

Coupling that with the blatant inspection she'd given his body, Linc had every right to expect she'd give him a warm welcome. Even at the restaurant, up until he'd figured out where she'd first seen him, she'd enjoyed every minute of his company. Before that, she had felt quite safe, had flirted outrageously and had actually been pleased when he'd begun to flirt back. She'd been playing a foolish game, but now it was his turn and he was planning to score.

Resigned to the confrontation that lay ahead, Chandra slowed down and came to a stop before reaching the fork in the road. Getting out of her car, she leaned back against the door, grateful for the night and the shadows of the surrounding, dense forest that further obscured her strained features. What she had to say was not going to be easy, but if they were going to be working together, it had to be said. When his headlights were a few yards down the road, she began waving her arms.

As expected, Linc stopped right behind her car, switched off his lights and got out of his truck. "What's the trouble?" he inquired as he walked to where she was standing.

"Look." Chandra took a deep breath and began talking in a no-nonsense tone. "Just because I watched you go skinny-dipping the other day is no reason for you to think that I want to have an affair with you. I realize that the way I acted when we met this morning might have given you that idea, but that's not how I feel. I'm not the kind of woman who takes one look at a naked man and has the instant desire to go to bed with him. I'm sorry you got that impression."

Chandra heard him clear his throat, preparing to speak, but she thought they'd both be far better off if he said nothing to make matters worse. She was willing to shoulder all the blame for what had gone on between them today. He could extricate himself quite gracefully from the situation if he just let it go at that. "Now I'd appreciate it if you'd get back in your truck and go home. We'll pretend today never happened and start fresh in the morning. From now on, we can be strictly business associates."

"How many looks would it take?" Linc asked softly.

"What?" Chandra blinked in confusion, not understanding the question.

"You said it would take more than one look at a naked man before you'd want to go to bed with him." Linc settled himself beside her, his hip grazing hers as he leaned back on her car. "How many times will I have to strip off my clothes before you'll want to go to bed with me?"

Sensing correctly that his question would bring about an instantaneous need on her part to put a great deal more space between them, Linc pushed away from the car and stood directly in front of her to prevent her from moving. "Twice? Three times?" he asked curiously, as he placed both hands on the car door at either side of her shoulders. Moonlight glanced off the gold streaks in his hair and shimmered in his blue eyes as he stared down into her stunned face.

Chandra sensed the laughter he was struggling to hold back and lost the last scrap of her composure. "Don't be ridiculous! I can understand your need to get back at me for embarrassing you in front of the other executives this morning, but you're going too far. And it's not all my fault. If it had been the other way around you would have acted the same way. You had most of your clothes off before I could tell you I was there. It was a shock running into you again this morning and I behaved badly. I'm sorry."

Then, for good measure, she added, "I could have had you arrested for trespassing, you know, but I didn't. As far as I'm concerned, we've both got our kicks out of this situation and it's time to lay it to rest in an adult manner. Now we're even."

"You're wrong," Linc observed smoothly, taking a small step closer, his arms keeping her trapped where she was. "If it had been the other way around, I would have taken off my clothes too and joined you in the lake."

His tone changed, becoming very low and husky as he went on. "You're a very intelligent woman and you look sophisticated but you appear to be somewhat naive. I'm afraid there are very few members of my sex who wouldn't have taken advantage of a situation like that were the roles reversed, or one like this."

"What do you mean, one like this?" Chandra murmured defensively as her heart began racing and her knees went weak.

Linc's eyes focused on her small, rosebud mouth. "A beautiful woman who has been coming on to me all day has just flagged me down in the middle of nowhere. There's nothing to prevent me from taking a sample of what you've been offering."

With that, he pulled her against him and lowered his head to her startled lips. He kissed her thoroughly, invading her soft mouth with the full thrust of his tongue. He stroked the delicate insides of her lips, delving deeper and deeper inside as she opened herself to him in involuntary invitation. It was like a microcosmic act of love and her response to the pleasure made her head swim. When she could no longer control the spiraling feelings that escalated faster and faster, she found herself melting against him.

It was then, after she had revealed the full extent of her desire for him, that he reached for the handle of the car door, opened it and guided her speechless, quivering body into a seated position behind the steering wheel.

Staring down into her luminous dark eyes, he berated her gently. "See? You really don't know me very well. For all you know, I might make a habit of taking advantage of lone women on deserted roads. I hope you don't take this kind of chance often. If you do, one day somebody might take more than a kiss. You're a beautiful woman and you should be more careful."

He started to walk away but then turned back. He pointed down the left fork in the road. "You can't see the house I'm building from Henry's place but it's about fifty yards farther down the road. I wasn't following you, Chandra, I was just driving home. As it happens, we're neighbors. I'm sure that does about as much for your peace of mind right now as it does for mine. In that way, we're even—for all the good it does us."

AT THREE IN THE MORNING, Linc gave up trying to sleep and rolled out of bed. After pulling on a pair of jeans, he opened the sliding door and stepped out onto the redwood deck. Staring into the dark night, he caught a distant glimmer of light through the trees. He knew it came from Chandra's cabin and blamed himself for her inability to sleep.

How the hell was he going to face her in the morning after what he'd done to her tonight? She had every right to be blazingly angry. Who did he think he was anyway? Whatever possessed him to grab her and kiss her like that? He knew very well, but it had taken more than five hours of restless tossing and turning before he could be honest with himself about it.

Chandra had got to him, really got to him, like no woman since Jean. As soon as he'd confirmed that she had spied on him and knew he was on to her, his negative feelings about her had died a rapid death. With a little suggestive teasing, he had learned she was not nearly as self-assured or aggressive as she'd first led him to believe. The dinner couldn't have ended quickly enough for her and she had wanted to race out of the restaurant as fast as she'd sped out of the parking lot.

He had suspected that the sight of his headlights behind her would shake her up a bit, though he hadn't expected her to stop her car in the middle of the road. Then, when she'd got out to confront him and given that indignant little speech, he'd been overwhelmed by a desire so strong it was painful. Knowing there was nothing she could have done to stop him if he'd acted on that feeling had frightened him more than he cared to admit. He'd kissed her mainly because he'd imagined doing it all day.

In all fairness to himself, he really had been concerned about her. He'd wanted to show her the possibly disastrous consequences of getting out of her car, after dark, in the middle of nowhere to angrily confront a man she knew next to nothing about. For some reason, even with her wild gypsy hair and sultry features, he thought of her as being terribly innocent.

On the other hand, the stronger hand, he had wanted to feel her sweet body squirming in his arms as he claimed the petal softness of her lips. He had kissed her, but her mouth had been only one small part of what he'd wanted to claim, especially once she'd started to respond. After that, it had taken more willpower than he'd thought he possessed to set her away from him.

It was crazy. *He* was crazy for even considering an involvement with her. She was a career woman to her Gucci-clad toes, with the polish of a social butterfly. Yet her rather Victorian reaction to his knowing she'd seen him nude had revealed that she was not the barracuda he had first thought. It followed that she also wasn't the type to indulge in a brief affair. Unfortunately, anything more than that would be impossible for him. She would fit into his life like a square peg in a round hole.

Raking one hand through the thickness of his hair, Linc went back inside. Needing to remind himself of his priorities, he walked down the hall and opened the door to a large bedroom. It was the first room in the house he had finished. Three twin beds with matching plaid twill spreads stood out from the paneled walls. He had built tall bookcases beside each bed, which not only served as room dividers but held the priceless treasures of three young boys.

Sitting down on the nearest bed, he thoughtfully fingered the collection of wooden animals on the nearby shelf. He picked up a carved bear cub, smiling to himself as he thought how much it resembled its owner. At eight, Chas was as rambunctious, curious and playful as a young bear. His snappy brown eyes and unruly black hair were so like his father's.

The smile on Linc's face faded. He squeezed his eyes shut, remembering his best friend Joseph Raincloud. Joe had been like a brother to him, and Linc still found it hard to believe that he was gone. They had met while trying out for the junior-high football team and had soon become inseparable. For their remaining years in school, Linc had been quarterback and Joe his best receiver. They had formed a winning combination off the field as well, collecting girls and racing trophies alike.

Neither Linc's family nor Joe's had ever tried to stand in the way of their friendship. Joe had been as welcome at the Young's farm as Linc had been at Henry's cabin in the woods. The summer after graduation from high school, Linc and Joe had traveled the amateur racing circuit together, but in the fall Linc had used his winnings to enroll in college. Joe had never considered going that route. His dream was to turn pro and amass a fortune from winning big-time motorcycle races.

For the next six years, while Linc worked to attain an advanced degree in business, Joe stayed on the circuit. He'd married a lovely girl he'd met at one of the local meets and thereafter his winnings had been used to support his young wife, Rebecca, and their growing family.

Joe's phenomenal driving skills had put him on the road to the top of his profession and he might one day have been deemed the best motorcyclist in the world. Unfortunately, before fame and financial security had been achieved, fate had stepped in. On a flight to an upcoming race, their small plane had gone down. Joe, Rebecca and their eldest son, Joe Jr., had been killed. By some miracle, the three youngest children had not been on board. Suffering from the flu, they had been left behind with a baby-sitter.

As he had done so many times since that day, Linc silently swore. It wasn't fair! Joe should be here to enjoy these boys, to see what fine men they would grow up to be. He'd have been so proud of them.

Linc could only hope he was raising them the way their father would have. It wasn't easy. He'd already lost a wife in the process, a wife who couldn't handle the responsibility of three rambunctious children suddenly being dropped in her lap. When Joe's will had named Linc guardian, Jean had been incredulous.

Linc took charge of the boys immediately after the accident. Jean had understood that action but had assumed they would have custody only until a suitable relative stepped forward to claim them. Even before the reading of the will, Linc had known that wasn't very likely. Rebecca's family had not approved of her marriage to an Indian and had had nothing to do with her since the day she'd eloped with Joe. That left Henry but he'd been getting on in years and lacked the financial means to support the boys.

Within a month, Jean had demanded Linc make a choice, and he'd made the only one his conscience would allow. He and the boys had moved out. Linc had never been sorry for making that decision. Even before the boys had arrived, his marriage had been on shaky ground. In the five years he and Jean had been together, he had come to realize that their relationship was primarily built on physical attraction. He had married her before he'd really got to know her and later learned they had little in common.

He wanted children. Jean did not. He wanted to get back to amateur racing but Jean threatened to walk out on him if he did. She felt that racing motorcycles was stupid and immature, a sport taken up by juvenile men who felt they continually had to prove their masculinity. They had frequent fights on the subject but Linc could never convince her that his love of speed and the excitement of racing posed little danger if a man took the right safety precautions. Jean refused to believe that a skilled biker was safer taking a high jump than most people were when driving their cars down the highway.

In the end, however, it had been Jean's career that had brought them to an impasse. It had been more important to her than anything else. Even though Linc hired a woman to help out with the boys, Jean refused to combine her work as a contract attorney with the responsibilities of raising a large family. One day she announced that she just couldn't feel any affection for children who were not her own and wanted them gone. In addition, she couldn't stand the constant noise or the clutter they made in her well-ordered house or the normal demands the three growing boys put upon her time. Less than a year after the divorce, she had married a colleague, fifteen years her senior, and the two of them were currently living in that picture-perfect house of hers.

Linc gazed at the clutter across the room and shook his head. Ten-year-old Ted had far more important things on his mind than picking up his belongings. The boy's nonexistent housekeeping skills would have driven Jean right up the wall. She had never understood Ted's need to save everything he'd ever owned or his penchant for animals. That thought reminded Linc that he hadn't fed the goldfish or the hamster or the guinea pig since Sunday morning.

He walked to the aquarium and sprinkled in a portion of powdered food, feeling guilty when the school of fish swiftly rose to the surface and devoured it all in seconds. As if they knew they too were finally going to be fed, the hamster began scratching on the walls of his cage and the guinea pig set up a whistling chatter. Linc filled their food dishes and reached in to scratch the guinea pig's back.

"Don't rat on me, fella. I promised Ted I'd take good care of you but those union negotiations went on all last night. Don't worry, Ted wil be home tomorrow and you'll be back to three squares a day."

He turned away and walked to the last bed, grateful he didn't have to feed the menagerie that resided there. He had yet to learn how Matt managed to sleep with all those stuffed animals taking up most of the bed. The boy was only four but still he required some room and there wasn't an inch of vacant space on the spread. Matt had adopted every hand-me-down stuffed toy his older brothers had discarded and no one could get him to part with any one of them.

Linc knew that Matt surrounded himself with soft, cuddly things partly because he could never get enough cuddling himself. Matt had been just a year old when Linc had become his only parent and though he'd done his best, the little guy had needed the softness of a woman's touch. In the past few months he had taken to asking interminable questions about mothers and had come to the conclusion that he wanted one for himself. Linc was waiting for the day when Matt would walk up to a likely-looking candidate and ask her if she was available for the position. He could just imagine how a woman like Chandra would react to a question like that.

Linc turned out the light in the boys' room and walked back down the hall. He looked at the rumpled covers of his empty bed and an overwhelming sense of loneliness settled over him. Three years, three years he had been without a woman but tonight was the first time he had really felt the void.

Although he knew Chandra Collins wasn't for him, Linc was also fully cognizant of the fact that she was the reason for his sudden attack of melancholy. He could almost see her curvaceous body reclining on his bed, picture the soft glow in her beautiful, dark eyes as he began kissing the sweet, delectable mouth that had been beckoning to him all day. She wanted him. He knew that. He also knew that their lovemaking would be wondrously fulfilling.

"Damn!" Linc groaned and swiveled on his heal. He couldn't afford to indulge in fantasies like that. Chandra was just as much a career woman as Jean had been, perhaps more so. After all, she was a partner in her own firm, had worked long and hard to achieve her reputation. Why would she want to get involved in a situation like his? If she ever witnessed the frequent total mayhem of his household, saw the boys in action, she would turn around and run the other way as fast as Jean had.

Being rational, Linc realized that would be Chandra's reaction, but he also knew how much effort it was going to take on his part to remember it. Logic had little to do with how he felt toward the woman, especially knowing she was going to be living right next door. Whenever he thought about her watching him as he'd stripped off his riding leathers, a thought he'd been having continually all night, he became aroused. If she didn't decide to move into a hotel for the remainder of her stay, he was going to be hard put not to do something foolish.

5

CHANDRA GLANCED AT THE CLOCK hanging on the wall behind Linc's desk—nine-thirty. She wondered if he was often late for work or if he hadn't come in yet because he wanted to avoid facing her after what had happened between them last night. She didn't know about him but she'd got very little sleep because of that all-consuming kiss and today she felt very much like a limp rag.

After another half hour, Chandra had to remind herself that she wasn't being paid to watch a clock but to conduct an audit. She picked up a red pencil and looked down at the first column of numbers in the ledger on her desk. They'd exchanged a simple kiss—nothing more. It probably hadn't meant a thing to Linc so it shouldn't to her. There was absolutely no reason to be nervous about seeing him again.

Unfortunately, even telling herself that she had no reason to feel the slightest trepidation did her no good. Her heartbeat went out of control whenever she heard someone walk past the office door, which was every twenty seconds. She couldn't forget the heated sensations Linc had caused in her body, couldn't forget how she'd responded to him when, ostensibly, all he'd been trying to do was make a point concerning her personal safety. What was she going to say to him when he came in? It had to be something infinitely sophisticated and wonderfully witty.

As she had done for hours the night before, Chandra tried to think of an appropriate speech that would put the incident in its proper perspective. She wanted to say something to relieve any tension between them so they could work comfortably together and forget about their initial reactions to each other.

She had to make Linc see that there was nothing personal between them, even though she had responded passionately to his kiss. She would tell him that she'd been working much too hard lately and had simply overreacted. She would lie through her teeth.

At ten-thirty, when Linc finally did arrive, sporting the smile of a man without a care in the world, Chandra was a frazzled wreck, totally irked by his beatific expression. "Even bankers aren't lucky enough to have your kind of hours," she bit out waspishly, then immediately regretted the outburst. He didn't work for her and she had no right to berate him, no matter how late he had chosen to come in or how she personally felt about him.

Linc's smile didn't fade one iota as he announced, "The union signed a contract at nine this morning. No walkout. Isn't that great?"

"I imagine it is," Chandra allowed in a far less hostile tone, but her mind wasn't on his good news and she had completely forgotten her intention to clear the air. She could hardly believe her own eyes. Linc was dressed in an expensive, lightweight, dove-gray suit that put her beige-and-white polka-dot linen ensemble to shame.

When he took off his jacket and hung it on a rack by the door, she saw that his shirt was snow-white and didn't show a single crease. The European tailoring hugged his well-developed torso and accentuated his broad shoulders. His striped tie was obviously pure silk and matched the handkerchief she had noticed peeking out of his breast pocket. Not one hair on his head was out of place.

Chandra was still trying to fathom this amazing transformation when Linc walked to his desk, sat down and opened the middle drawer. He pulled out a leather case, extracted his glasses and put them on, then replaced the case in the drawer.

"I left a list of inventory terminology on your desk when I got in this morning. If you don't have any questions about it, Chandra, I've got a lot of work to catch up on. I've let a number of things slide during these negotiations. I was beginning to think we'd never come to an agreement and I'd end up buried under a ton of unfinished paperwork."

He accepted her silence at face value and pulled a sheaf of papers from one of the files stacked on his desk. A moment later, he was completely engrossed in his work. In a daze, Chandra looked at her desk and saw the paper she hadn't spotted before, but that wasn't what caused the dumbfounded stare she threw at the man who had delivered it. Finally, a burning curiosity got the better of her. "This is quite a change from yesterday. Will the real Lincoln Young please stand up."

"Hmm?" Linc asked absentmindedly, not lifting his eyes from the papers.

"I was wondering what brought about this change

in your appearance. Yesterday you were dressed like a recruit from the Salvation Army. The day before that you looked like a member of some motorcycle gang and today you look like an international financier. Do you have any other disguises I should be aware of?"

It was the first time since she'd overheard him exchanging words with a pair of loons that he'd emitted that unbridled laugh of pure enjoyment. The sound of it did dangerous things to Chandra's libido and she was afraid it might show in her bemused expression. She bit her lip, hoping the small pain would sidetrack the flaming responses beginning to speed through her body. After yesterday there was no way she was going to reveal in look, word or deed that she thought him the most attractive man she'd ever seen.

"Well?" She forced out the question in what she hoped was an even tone.

"That depends on what you consider a disguise," Linc began, his blue eyes sparkled with amusement though his expression was thoughtful. "When I'm working on my house, I usually wear jeans, a long-sleeved shirt and boots. Most other times I put on whatever's comfortable. At work I dress as you see me today unless I've been talking to a representative of the local union like Stan Olson. He has this fierce mistrust of management, so I wear something like that old suit I had on yesterday. I know I looked sort of rumpled but that was because Stan and I talked all night and I needed a nap before coming into the office. I snatched a couple of hours in the back of my truck."

"And you only need glasses for reading, not for

measuring distance when you decide it might be fun to jump your motorcycle off a cliff or tear around the trunks of a few trees," Chandra concluded, relieved of the anxiety she'd felt when she'd seen that her daredevil sported horn-rimmed glasses.

"My, my. You were watching me for quite some time, weren't you?" Linc removed his glasses. He dangled them in one hand as he stared across the room at her. "When I'm studying figures I rely on these to prevent eyestrain. I don't need them to see you and so far the strain that's causing has nothing to do with my eyes."

He focused on her face, grinning at her open mouth. "You've got hair the color of dark toffee, tender lips like a delicate rose and fawnlike eyes."

She wasn't prepared to deal with his unexpected compliments. The kiss he had delivered last night had been meant to teach her a lesson and she had learned one all right. Caution was the byword where Lincoln Young was concerned. She was more susceptible to him than to a virulent virus. "A man doesn't need glasses to say something like that," she asserted with commendable aplomb.

"Very well. You shouldn't try to cover that tiny mole on your right cheek with makeup," he chided teasingly. "It's really quite cute."

Instantly Chandra brought her hand up to the slight imperfection she'd thought was completely concealed but immediately lowered it again when she saw Linc's triumphant smirk. "All right, I'll concede that you have sufficiently good vision to drive a motorcycle without jeopardizing your health."

"Were you worried about me, Chandra?" His

voice held a seductive lure but she had no intention of taking the bait.

"I don't know you well enough to worry about you," Chandra shot back, looking down at the ledger that lay open on her desk. "I just didn't want to wake up some morning and find your body washed up on my beach."

She ignored his soft chuckle and tried to concentrate on the numbers in front of her but she was more aware of him than ever. It was as though the self-conscious, rumpled-looking man of the previous day had totally ceased to exist and in his place was a self-assured, worldly, well-groomed executive vice-president of finance. Chandra wasn't so sure she liked the change and was even less certain that she could resist the man if he continued to behave along these enervating new lines.

Chandra needn't have worried about Linc's behavior toward her, however. The atmosphere of intimacy he'd created hadn't lasted more than a few minutes and after the suggestive comments he'd made upon his arrival, he'd been all business for the rest of that day. To make matters even more confusing, each day thereafter was much the same. Since he never digressed from matters pertaining to the company, Chandra saw no need to ward him off. It was as if the kiss they'd shared had never happened.

It appeared he could turn those seductive powers of his on and off at will, and where Chandra was concerned he'd chosen to turn them off. Although she tried to tell herself that she didn't care, it bothered her that one moment he had looked at her as if she was the most desirable woman in the world and in the next had forgotten she was there. Evidently he had satisfied his curiosity, then written her off. She felt both relieved and frustrated.

While going over the minutes of past board meetings, Chandra discovered that Linc was responsible for most of the innovative ideas Hammond Paper had instituted to increase their profits during the past year. She had to admire the system of internal checks and controls he had installed and his efficient design of a cost system of accounting. Conducting the audit for Hammond would be relatively easy, for Chandra could already see that the financial records of the company were kept in accordance with acceptable principles of accounting. It was going to be a simple matter to confirm the accuracy of the data. All she would have to do once she'd reviewed any matters pertaining to the financial condition of the company was to contact the debtors, creditors and banks that dealt with Hammond and supervise a physical inventory.

By the end of the week, Chandra and Linc had established a work routine that made it very clear to Chandra that her attraction to Linc had no future. They shared the same office, often spent long hours discussing contracts and bond indentures, but she was unable to draw him into any conversation of a personal nature. The one time she had forced the issue and inquired about his motivation for riding a motorcycle in what she thought was a reckless manner, he'd cleverly sidestepped the question. He did assure her that he would not ride his bike on her property but that was all she was able to get out of him. Indeed, his frigid blue eyes had revealed that he didn't appreciate her bringing up a subject that didn't pertain to business.

Chandra had known all along that it was foolish to get involved with an employee of a client. She should have been grateful that Linc seemed to want to forget all about that first day. But she wasn't. Being treated strictly as a business associate by a gorgeous man whose kiss had shaken her to the very core of her being was enough to make her question her femininity. What had she done to make him turn off like that?

Several times as they'd shared a quick lunch in the cafeteria or worked together past closing, Chandra had thought she might rekindle the desirous flames she'd seen in his eyes the night he had kissed her, but it had never happened. In fact he rarely looked at her at all, at least not that she could see. He never made a comment when she wore a particularly flattering dress or styled her hair differently. Eventually Chandra had to admit that he probably just didn't notice and that thought depressed her more than anything.

By Friday Chandra was anxious for the weekend to begin so she would have two days to convince herself that it didn't matter what Linc thought of her and that she was a fool for continuing to hope he might start something. He'd lost interest and that was that. She had to accept it and stop making herself miserable.

After lunch she put in a call to her partner, who knew her too well not to sense her mood. "What's wrong, Chandra?" Karen asked. "Don't the numbers add up?"

"The audit is going fine. Thad Hammond is a dear, and for the most part his executives have been very helpful. I might even finish up early."

"Do I detect a bit of hostility there, Chandra?" Karen probed. "Is one of Hammond's executives giving you a hard time?"

"I'm not even getting the time of day," Chandra blurted, then told Karen all that had occurred since she'd arrived at her cabin, ending with, "He's so damned sexy he could burn your socks off with one look from those gorgeous blue eyes. Unfortunately, he has no desire to look my way."

Karen mixed the right amount of sympathy with her usual measure of cynicism toward the male of the species. "If he can't recognize a good thing when he sees it, then he's not worth your interest. Finish the audit and come home, Chandra. I've found this incredibly handsome dentist who is dying to meet you."

"With my luck, he'll probably take one look at me and find the only thing that interests him is my overbite," Chandra declared somewhat churlishly but then admitted that Karen was probably right. Any man who made a woman feel like one of the ugly stepsisters didn't deserve another thought. She had too much pride to lust after someone who didn't have any interest in her.

Chandra was laughing by the time she ended the call. "I'll get in touch next week and tell you when I'm free for my next dental appointment."

LINC STOPPED HIS CAR at the parking lot exit, waiting to pull onto the highway. The rain was coming down in sheets. "Visibility can't be more than two feet," he muttered in disgust.

He glanced in his rearview mirror. Chandra's

rental car was still in its assigned slot. "Oh hell!" He threw the gears into reverse and began backing up.

There was no getting around it. He couldn't leave her behind in weather like this. No matter how many times he told himself he was not responsible for her welfare, Linc's stride never wavered as he made his way through the driving rain toward the building. The woman had interrupted his sleep enough this past week. He'd be damned if he was going to lose any more. Unless he made sure she was home safe and sound, he wouldn't even get a wink.

You need a shrink! Linc berated himself as he pushed open the door and marched down the back hall. *If you're not lusting after her, you're worrying about her!*

He didn't know what it was about her but he was constantly plagued by an urge to protect her. He'd warned the company lecher, Turner, to stay away from her, checked up on her place every night to assure himself all was well and even found himself making certain she never skipped lunch. What business was it of his if she wanted to starve herself away to nothing? After all, she was thirty years old and had managed just fine without him so far.

He paused at the door to his office. How was she going to react to this sudden show of paternal concern on his part? He could almost picture her thumbing her nose at his offer to see her safely home. All week he'd done his best to make her think his only interest in her was within the context of her position as their auditor. If he walked through that door, she wouldn't believe that for another minute.

Maybe he could disrupt her thinking with some

fancy footwork. The best defense was a good offense and he could be pretty offensive if he put his mind to it. If he made her mad enough, maybe she'd overlook the fact that he was behaving like a besotted fool.

CHANDRA HAD HOPED TO LEAVE THE OFFICE by five but it was almost seven before she finished running numbers on a stack of contracts Hammond had signed with several suppliers. She assumed that Linc had left early since she hadn't seen him since three that afternoon and was astonished when he stormed into the office just as she was reaching for her purse.

"What the devil are you still doing here?" he demanded.

Chandra's brows rose at the rude tone of his question and the condition of his clothing. He was soaking wet! "I'm just leaving. I thought you had already gone."

"Well I hope you've got an umbrella with you," Linc replied cuttingly, shaking a shower of raindrops from his hair. "Otherwise, you're going to get as wet as I am. This thing shows no sign of letting up."

Since there weren't any windows in Linc's office, Chandra had been unaware of a change in the weather. When she'd gone out to lunch with Marge, the sun had been shining. "I didn't even know it was raining."

"I gathered that when I saw your car was still here," he said in a vexed tone that intensified as he went on. "Don't you realize what kind of drive you've got in store for you because of this weather?"

Adjusting the strap of her purse over one shoulder, she started for the door. "If I remember correctly, you've got the very same drive. Why haven't you started out before now?"

"Because I have a four-wheel-drive Bronco, not a small economy car that couldn't navigate a puddle. I was on my way out of the lot when I recognized your car. I thought you had better sense," he charged, unaware that Chandra was reevaluating the unfeeling attitude he'd shown her all week.

"I'll follow you home to make sure you don't end up in a ditch but next time you'd better think ahead. I'd hate to find your body wrapped around some tree on that slippery road up to your cabin."

"You were worried about me," she stated quietly.

Linc hid his wince at her insight. Taking a firm hold on her elbow, he herded her toward the door. "I'd be worried about anybody who had to make a forty-mile drive in this weather. That road to Willow Lake is well on its way to becoming a sea of mud. It'll be damned near impassable by the time we get there if we don't head out right now." He tightened his grip. "Come on. Let's get going."

Even though his clothes were completely soaked by the time they'd traversed the parking lot, Linc walked with Chandra to her car, where he unceremoniously stuffed her inside. "Don't start out until I'm behind you," he ordered and strode off in the rain toward his Bronco.

Over an hour later Chandra turned onto the winding road to the lake. As she'd done a number of times throughout the drive, she glanced in her rearview mirror and saw Linc's headlights gleaming through the driving rain. Unlike the last time he'd followed her, the sight of his truck behind her gave her a pleasant sense of security. It had been a long, miserable drive and several times they'd had to stop because the rain was so intense it had reduced visibility to the point where they couldn't see to go on.

Navigating the dirt road to the cabin was even more difficult than Chandra had thought it would be. Her knuckles were white as she gripped the steering wheel and her neck muscles were stiff with tension as she strained to keep the car on the muddy road. She couldn't drive too slow or her wheels would mire down in the mud, yet if she went too fast, she'd plane. At last, she saw the fork in the road that meant she had less than a mile to go.

She stepped down slightly on the accelerator, adjusting her speed to allow for the increased grade of the road. Without warning her back tires skidded sharply to the right and she couldn't compensate fast enough. The rear end of the car slid across the shoulder and the tires sank in the soft mud. It took only seconds for Chandra to realize that she was stuck.

"Damn, damn, damn," she muttered, pounding on the steering wheel with her fist.

It seemed that Linc had not wasted much time reaching the same conclusion when he appeared at the car door. Without hesitation, he pulled it open and hauled her outside. "We'll pull it out in the morning," he shouted to be heard above the rising wind. "I'm taking you the rest of the way."

"My purse and keys!" she shouted back.

Linc reached back into the car for her belongings and thrust them into her hands. "Here!"

They had gone only two steps before Linc realized that Chandra's high heels could cope with the mud

no better than her car. Not asking her permission, he
scooped her up in his arms. The distance between
their vehicles was short but they were exposed long
enough for the pelting rain to completely saturate
Chandra's clothes.

Her hair absorbed the water like a sponge and sent
rivulets of rain down her back. She wrapped her
arms around Linc's neck and turned her cheek into
his shoulder but his body provided little shelter. It
was as wet and cold as her own. She closed her eyes,
gritted her teeth and endured.

Linc had left his door open and set her down on
the seat before sliding in beside her. To make room
for him, she was forced to slither under the wheel
and across the slippery vinyl. The action twisted
the sodden silk of her shirtwaist around her legs
and the skirt worked its way up to midthigh. It was
almost impossible for Chandra to pull the cling-
ing material down; it stuck to her like a second
skin.

Chandra cast a nervous glance at Linc, bracing herself for the comment he was bound to make about the
expansive show of leg she'd just awarded him. She
needn't have worried. His features looked as if they
were cast in stone and his eyes were riveted on the
road ahead. He threw the Bronco into gear without
saying a word.

The heater was on but it did nothing to dispel the
icy chill that claimed her body. Shivering, Chandra
wrapped her arms about herself as much to keep
warm as to hide the revealing outline of her breasts
and taut nipples beneath the wet silk. She felt naked
but her condition seemed to have no effect on Linc.

Or so she thought, until she saw his granite expression break into a mocking grin.

"Now we're really even," he observed wolfishly. "You've got legs that just don't quit." His eyes moved to her arms that were attempting to hide the shape of her wet bosom. "Good try, but I saw those beautiful breasts too when I was carrying you."

Chandra was consumed by an unbearable heat. She looked down at herself, expecting to see steam rising from the twin curves he had just complimented. She could think of nothing to say and turned her attention to the rain-spattered window beside her, refusing to look at him during the remainder of the drive to her cabin. As soon as they stopped, she mumbled a hurried thank-you and reached for the door handle, desperately wanting to escape the potent sexual atmosphere that filled the interior of the vehicle.

"Don't you think you owe me a little something for giving you a ride home?" Linc drawled in a way that sent shivers down her spine.

Chandra refused to let herself be victimized by her own traitorous body. She was shivering enough from the cold and didn't need any help from Linc to aggravate her condition. "I said thank-you," she reminded him through chattering teeth. Then she made the mistake of looking at him and couldn't pull her eyes away when he started stripping off his shirt. "Wh-what are you doing?"

Bare-chested, he reached behind him for the blanket resting on the back seat. "I'm warmer without the shirt," he said as if that explained everything. "But you're turning blue."

One hand closed around her wrist and he drew her body away from the door. "This should help until you get into the house." He draped the blanket over her shoulders and wrapped it securely around her body. Without another word, he stepped outside, turned and, sliding her across the seat to his door, lifted her in his arms. This time he remembered her purse and tucked it inside the blanket before setting out. "Find your keys," he directed as he mounted the steps toward her front door.

Chandra fumbled inside her purse and was ready with the door key as soon as they reached the deck. Her fingers shook but she managed to get the door open.

Without putting her down, Linc stepped inside and closed the door with his foot. But as soon as he ventured to walk across the floor the smooth soles of his shoes slipped on the wet planking. In a vain attempt to keep from falling backward and forgetting for an instant the extra weight he was still carrying, he overcompensated and went facedown in the other direction. The breath was forced out of Chandra's lungs as they fell together, Linc's full weight on top of her.

"Did I hurt you? Did I hurt you?" Linc finally managed to get off her and dragged her limp body onto his lap. His hands rubbed up and down her spine as she gasped for air. Frantically, he got her out of the blanket and undid the top few buttons of her dress. "Chandra, I'm sorry. I didn't mean to fall on you. I couldn't stop myself." His words of abject apology poured forth as he scanned her ashen face.

"I . . . I'll be okay. Was an accident," she managed between coughs. In her anxiety to fill her lungs with air, she plucked at the material of her bodice. She was appalled when Linc assumed she was trying to undo more buttons and proceeded to help her.

At the feel of his warm fingers on her bare skin, she pushed at his hands, her breath completely restored, and protested, "Don't do that. I don't need any help."

Linc stifled a groan at the feel of her bottom wiggling around on his thighs. The desire he'd fought so hard to contain exploded within him. How could a man ignore the demands of his body when the woman he wanted was against him, her breasts completely exposed by the transparent wisp of a lace bra? The luscious curves were practically spilling into his hands, the nipples peaked with invitation.

When Chandra scooted off his lap, the back of one silken thigh stroked his burgeoning manhood. Provoked beyond endurance, Linc wrapped one arm around her waist and lowered her shoulders to the floor. Gazing down into her large brown eyes, he stretched out beside her and lowered his head. "I've had all of this I can take," he ground out thickly and his hungry mouth came down on her parted lips.

His tongue pressed deep into her mouth and set an erotic rhythm, plunging in and pulling out until Chandra willingly opened to him. The stimulation of his deep kiss was so powerful that she felt as if he truly were joining with her in the most intimate of embraces.

Chandra felt small and defenseless as he turned her pliant form until they were facing each other. She could feel every inch of him; the urgency in his body as he molded her against his length. The crisp hair on his chest created a tingling abrasion along the expanse of skin exposed by the open V of her bodice. Her hands came up and moved restlessly over his bare shoulders, her fingers wandered into the light, tawny hair at the back of his neck.

Linc made a low, animal sound in his throat as he fitted one palm over her breast and felt the hard thrust of her nipple. He was powerless to resist the demands of his own body and its instinctive urgings. Enflamed further by her soft moans, he undid the remaining buttons and spread wide the front of her dress. The center clasp of her bra was a fragile gate to the treasures beyond and it offered no resistance as he entered.

Linc began to tremble as his lips took their first taste of one dusky rosebud. Wild with need, he took her nipple deeply into his mouth, drawing the sweetness of her into himself. His free hand stroked up her thigh and cupped the rounded buttocks he'd admired for a week. His fingers splayed across the soft flesh, memorizing the feel of her as he pressed her to his hard arousal.

To Chandra, it seemed as if all her fantasies about him had converged into one overwhelming reality. His kisses, his touch, the pressure of his maleness against her belly, each was a possessive fusion. On every level but the final one, he mated with her. She arched her back and strained against the rigid invitation his body made to hers. She had yearned for the thrill of this moment for so long that she could think of nothing but what would inevitably happen if they continued this way. She wanted it to happen, needed it more than anything.

Boldly, wantonly, her hand slid between their

bodies to explore the essence of his maleness. She stroked him through the damp material, almost fainting with excitement at the sound of his ragged moans. Just when she was certain that she was truly going to learn what it felt like to be loved by this man, he emitted a harsh gasp and thrust himself away from her.

He was standing up and striding to the door before Chandra had assimilated his withdrawal. "I'm not an animal," he rasped in a tortured tone that told her he was not condemning her but himself. "I want you, Chandra, but I can't have you. I've got a good life, and if I take what you're offering I'll probably lose it. I can't take that chance."

6

CHANDRA'S BOOK LAY OPEN to the same page she had reached close to an hour earlier when she'd first curled up in the tufted fireside chair and started reading. Though her eyes were directed toward the print, her mind wouldn't assimilate the words. Despite the humiliation she had recently suffered, she drifted in a daydream far more fascinating than the love scene depicted in the book.

She didn't see the black-haired horseman described in the historical novel but a motorcyclist with light brown hair, warmly streaked by the sun. Azure eyes as clear and inviting as a Minnesota lake beckoned to her. His cool lips, fresh and damp from the rain, moved over her face, while his hands, their tops sprinkled with golden brown hair, moved lightly over her nakedness. His powerful body....

She shook herself, determined to eradicate this kind of longing once and for all. After last night, how could she possibly set herself up for more disappointment? She didn't understand Lincoln, never had, never would. Maybe he really did suffer from a split personality. Instinctively, she knew that the reckless biker in him wouldn't hesitate to make her fantasies a reality. But evidently the pedantic accountant in him lived by an entirely different set of rules. That side of Linc never took risks.

Even if that were the case, Chandra saw no reason for the harsh statement Linc had flung at her the night before. How could making love to her ruin his supposedly "good life"? Sensing the loneliness in him, the need that sometimes overwhelmed his caution, Chandra couldn't understand why he considered his life so good anyway.

Perhaps he thought all that was required for a good life was a total lack of female companionship. Maybe his ex-wife was responsible for his ambivalent attitude toward the opposite sex. Chandra knew he desired her but that he was determined to resist the feeling. It was as if she represented some kind of threat, but what possible threat could she be to him?

The thud of footsteps on the wooden stairs leading to her front door roused her from her depressing thoughts. The book fell to the rug as Chandra sprang to her feet. Linc! It had to be Lincoln.

Slowly, with great trepidation, Chandra walked to the door. What was he doing back here again? If he hadn't made it clear last night that he wanted nothing more to do with her, he certainly had this morning.

It had been before nine and she had just stepped out of the shower when she'd heard a rapping at the door. Belting her chenille robe around her damp body, Chandra had responded to the summons. Having forgotten all about his promise to deliver her car, she'd been surprised to see Linc standing on her deck. Naively hoping he had come to take back his cold dismissal of her and tell her he wanted to start anew, she'd invited him in for coffee.

He'd ignored her tentative smile and refused her polite offer. Instead, he'd coolly informed her that her car was no longer mired in the mud, then promptly handed her the keys. Barely waiting for a thank-you, he'd quickly turned and fled back down the steps. Chandra had been left standing in the doorway watching him jog down her driveway. He couldn't have been in more of a hurry to get away if she'd been a rabid skunk.

Chandra slid the door open slowly, hoping her expression showed idle disinterest and reflected none of her inner turmoil. She'd been so sure it would be Linc standing on the deck that it took a moment for her brain to identify the caller or, rather, callers. An older man with jet-black hair and eyes to match stood patiently staring down at her. Three young boys peeped out from behind him. Their hair and eyes were the same color as his but their expressions were full of wary curiosity.

"Henry? Henry Raincloud?" Chandra asked, though she'd already recognized her caretaker. It was years since she'd seen him but time had wrought little change in his hawklike features. The lines around his mouth and eyes were a bit deeper and his shoulders weren't quite as strong and straight as she remembered, but the laughter that always seemed to lurk within his dark irises was still there.

"Didn't know if you'd remember this old Injun," Henry quipped, the whispering smoothness of his voice unchanged by the years.

"I could never forget the man who taught me how to walk through the woods and listen to the songs of the wind," Chandra answered, delight sparkling from her warm brown eyes as she eagerly drank in Henry's features. She'd adored this gentle man and all the lessons he'd taught her over those long-ago summers. Each autumn she had awed her city friends with her knowledge of nature and Indian lore.

"That was a hard lesson for Little Talking Curls to learn," Henry remarked affectionately. "I hope she can still hear the music."

"A wise man once told me to use my heart and not my ears. He also said it was a wise child who remained quiet in the face of such wisdom."

"But Little Talking Curls was not always a wise child. She would chatter like the chipmunks. Now she is a woman."

The sparkle in Henry's eyes grew a tiny bit brighter but the line of his mouth remained straight as if the words he'd spoken were very solemn. Chandra remembered a lot of things about Henry, especially the sagelike demeanor he always adopted when in reality he was having a great time teasing her.

"You didn't grow too tall but enough not to be mistaken for a chipmunk," he finally judged. "It's good that you're back."

"I stayed away too long. I guess I've changed, at least a little, but you're still the same." Chandra chuckled. She blinked back the moisture in her eyes that had gathered at his use of the name he'd attached to her when she'd been hardly more than a chubby-legged toddler.

She stepped toward him, wanting to put her arms around this man who was her only link with such pleasant memories of the past. Instead, she clasped her hands together, recalling that physical displays of affection had always made him uncomfortable. "It's so good to see you again, Henry. Won't you come in?"

"Grandpa? Ask her about fishing?" the whispered voice came from behind Henry, pleading for attention.

"These handsome boys are your grandsons?" Chandra asked, extending a welcome smile to the three youngsters who'd been patiently quiet during her reunion with their grandfather. All three boys, nearly perfect stairsteps in height, nodded their heads in solemn confirmation.

The middle one stepped forward, proclaiming himself spokesman for the group. A bit shyly but with a great deal of dignity, he looked her straight in the face. Chandra guessed his age to be around eight or nine. "Will you let us fish in your lake, Miss Collins? We know it's private property but we promise not to make much noise."

Chandra was momentarily taken aback. "Of course you can fish in the lake. It doesn't belong to me but to everyone. Your grandfather taught me that lesson long ago. I own some of the land around the edge but even that should be shared."

"But Uncle Linc said that a city lady like you wouldn't want three boys like us bothering her and that we'd have to wait until you went away." The boy's words rushed out but then he looked embarrassed by the outburst.

Chandra turned to Henry in confusion but there were no explanations forthcoming from that quarter. For once, the man dropped his inscrutable facade and looked highly uncomfortable. The realization that

Uncle Linc had to be none other than Lincoln Young washed over Chandra. If he had been present she would have cheerfully wrung his neck. How could he have given these children such an unfair impression of her character?

"Your Uncle Linc doesn't really know me very well," she began, postponing her curious questions about the man's relationship with Henry's grandchildren. "This city lady happens to like to fish and likes to share that lake out there."

The eyes of all three boys grew a little wider as if stunned by her confession. Glaring over her shoulder to Henry who by now had pulled on his stoic expression, Chandra decided the elderly gentleman deserved to be included in her neck-wringing. Henry could easily have disabused the boys of the notion that she was such a fussbudget. Surely he hadn't thought she would have changed that much over the years.

"You know what?" she asked, waiting for the boys to shake their heads. "When I was a little girl, your grandfather showed me the best places to catch the biggest walleye in that lake."

"He did?" voiced the youngest boy, his dark eyes as big as saucers.

"He sure did and I still remember one of those places. Tell you what, if I bring along a sack of cookies I baked this morning, would you let me go fishing with you?" She looked from one boy to the other, noted their skepticism and guessed the reason behind it.

Grinning, she went on, "I promise to bait my own hook and remove my own catch. How about it?" For good measure she threw in an additional bribe. "You can taste the cookies first and see if they're worth letting a woman go fishing with you. They're sugar cookies with lemon frosting."

The spokesman for the trio looked first to his brothers as if gathering their votes. After receiving their almost imperceptible nods, he directed his attention to his grandfather who gave his. "Okay, you can come too."

"Thanks," Chandra said and offered her hand. "By the way, my name's Chandra, what's yours?"

"I'm Charles," the boy announced as he grasped her hand and gave it a surprisingly firm shake. Brushing a lock of unruly black hair away from his forehead, he declared, "You can call me Chas—everybody else does."

"I'm very happy to meet you, Chas." She looked to the tallest, who appeared to be about ten. "And you are?"

"Ted. . .Theodore Raincloud," he furnished and also grasped her hand, briefly but firmly. His soft brown eyes conveyed shyness and a gentle nature much different from that of his more gregarious younger brother.

"And I'm Matt." The youngest, a cherub-faced preschooler, pushed forward to introduce himself. Unlike Ted's dignified greeting, Matt pumped her hand enthusiastically, his chubby fingers as soft as a babe's.

Chandra grinned at Henry. "After all that rain last night, do you think we'll have much luck out there?"

"Sunfish always bite."

Henry's reply was brief and she knew there would be no elaboration. Stepping back into the house to gather what she needed for the fishing expedition, Chandra chuckled to herself. Henry's remarks were always that brief unless accompanied by his impromptu "wise old Indian sayings."

Trying to keep a straight face during Henry's colorful dissertations had been a game she and her parents had played with him each summer. Beautifully phrased words of wisdom would flow from Henry's mouth as easily as a river over a waterfall. The creative Indian seemed to have an appropriate homespun philosophy for almost every incident.

She wondered now if Henry spun his sayings out for his grandsons or if those had been entertainment reserved for the babbling little white girl, an outsider. As she recalled, he used to have her hanging on his every word. She'd been thrilled to be privy to his secret and supposedly ancient teachings. Maybe his grandsons weren't so gullible concerning the nebulous discourses of the Great Spirit.

Thinking of the boys, she turned around and was disappointed when they weren't right behind her. She'd thought sampling her cookies would have been enough of an enticement for them to follow her, drop a few of the barriers she sensed they'd erected against her. Chandra didn't know a great deal about children but what little she did know made her sure their quiet patience during her reunion with Henry wasn't their usual behavior.

Boys their ages were normally so high on the pure joy of living that they were whirlwinds of perpetual motion and nonstop chatter. Maybe sugar cookies with lemon icing didn't appeal to them. Chandra leaned against the counter, munching one of the questionably delicious cookies. No, it wasn't the cookies, she was sure. She'd used her mother's recipe, one she and all of her friends had loved when they'd been children. There had to be some other reason for the boys' reluctance to come inside.

They appeared to be bright, sparkling-eyed youngsters. Their sturdy little bodies exuded health and vigor. Indians, even the children, often demonstrated a reticence around outsiders, Chandra knew, but sensed there was more to it than that. Oh no! She nearly choked on the last bite of her cookie as she went in search of Henry.

Finding him, all alone, leaning against the rail around the deck, she asked, "Where are the boys?"

"Digging for worms," he answered, pointing to the clearing near the boat house. Sure enough, Chas and Matt were studying each spadeful of earth Ted turned over. Their excited voices and squeals of glee each time a fat wiggling worm was discovered and dropped into a waiting bucket could be heard even from this distance. It confirmed her suspicions.

"Henry, please be honest with me. Have I pushed my way in on a special outing with your grandsons? I don't know how often you see them and maybe they'd really rather not have a stranger tagging along. I'll understand, really I will. I don't want to ruin the day for them and I didn't mean to intrude."

"I see those boys every day and we go fishing all the time," Henry said, correcting her misassumption. In a rare moment of expansion, he went on, "They're not used to being around women. My son Joe, his wife and their oldest boy were killed three years ago...." Henry paused and Chandra saw the pain of a great loss reflected in his expression.

"Oh Henry, I'm so sorry." Chandra's voice was hushed and she didn't refrain from touching him this time. Feeling his grief, she laid her hand gently on his shoulder, letting him know she understood the loss of someone deeply loved. "I remember Joe. He didn't come over here very often but I liked him."

Henry acknowledged her condolences with a slight nod of his head, meeting her gaze. In that moment, they shared the mutual pain of losing their families. "The boys live with Linc now," Henry said after a few moments. "He is their legal guardian but I watch over them when he's working."

"Lincoln Young is raising those boys?" Chandra was astounded, her dark eyes growing nearly as large as the boys' had when she'd told them she liked to fish. Was there no end to the varying facets of Lincoln Young? No wonder he was building a house way out here in the country. It was a perfect place to raise three growing boys and at the same time keep them close to their grandfather who would never be confined to the city.

Henry nodded his head, then quietly said, "Linc and my boy Joe were very good friends. There was no one else who wanted to take my grandsons into their life. Linc was the only one who would make room in his heart for them. Joe knew that and trusted him to make men out of his sons."

"But Henry, they're such beautiful children," Chandra said, struck by a surge of compassion. "Anyone would want them." How fortunate Joe's children were that they had a grandfather and their father's closest friend to love them after their parents had died. She felt a slight twinge of jealousy.

When she had lost her parents and gone to live with her aunt and uncle, she had also lost the freedom to be herself. Rachel and Harold Collins had tried their best but had been too old to understand the normal exuberance of a high-spirited young girl. Over the years, she had formed a shell of artificial reserve that hadn't cracked until she'd returned to this cabin.

There were so many questions she wanted to have answered about Linc and the Raincloud children. What about their mother's family? Why hadn't they come forward to take charge of the boys? Surely their maternal grandparents could have provided the boys with a more natural family structure. She could almost feel the lack of a motherly influence in Joe's children. "How could anyone not want those adorable boys?" she repeated as much to herself as to Henry.

His answer was a slight shrug of his shoulders, then, "Not all people have an open spirit, Talking Curls. You come and fish with us. It will be good for them and for you."

THE AFTERNOON SUN GLITTERED across the lake's smooth surface. The silver canoe with its three occupants, Henry, Ted and Chas, floated quietly out in the middle of the bay. Chandra watched with envy as Henry slipped a net under Ted's catch. That had to be the tenth sunfish or crappie she'd seen them land. Henry and the other boys were having far more luck than she and little Matt.

At the last minute Chandra and Matt had elected to fish from the dock, sure they'd have more luck there, but so far they hadn't got so much as a nibble. She knew from Matt's deep sighs that he was growing more and more dispirited. It hadn't been a total loss, however. Their sack of cookies was nearly gone, most of them having disappeared into Matt's cherubic mouth. She'd also managed to get him talking and had learned quite a bit about Matt's brothers, their pets—and their "Uncle Linc."

Chandra swished her toes across the top of the water, wondering how Linc would react to Matt's suggestion that she teach his "uncle" how to make cookies. "He cooks pretty good spaghetti," the boy had said. "But I don't think he knows much about cookies or cakes."

Chandra had countered with the suggestion that she teach Matt how to bake but he'd looked at her as if she'd suddenly gone daft. "I'm too little, you know."

He was but she knew he'd have a lot of fun helping. He was also too little for a lot of other things—especially for being so serious. Chandra's arms ached to scoop him up on her lap and teach him silly songs, do something to bring out the giggles she wanted to hear him voice. Maybe some other time, she thought. For now, she would have to content herself with sitting quietly beside him, gratified that at least he didn't appear uncomfortable around her any longer.

"It went under!" Matt pointed excitedly at the spot where his red-and-white bobber had disappeared.

The line was spinning out from the reel, indicating a fish had taken the bait. At least Chandra hoped it was a fish. With the violence of the storm the night before, walleyes and northerns wouldn't be biting and sunfish or crappies wouldn't run with the bait like whatever was at the other end of Matt's fishing line. It seemed more likely the catch was one of the many snapping turtles that swam near the shore and under the dock. Still, she wasn't about to put a damper on Matt's enthusiasm. There was always a chance that one of the bigger fish had gone against the norm and struck the bait even though the water had been churned up by a heavy rain.

"Careful now," she cautioned and put her arm around him, unobtrusively slowing the whirling handle. Guiding Matt's pudgy hand to the crank, she instructed, "Reel him in. Slow now, we don't want to lose him." She kept her own hand just over his in case the fish decided to struggle. After all, Matt was only four years old and didn't have the strength of his older brothers.

"We got one! We got one!" Matt squealed with excitement.

"You sure did, partner," Chandra praised. "Looks like it might be a keeper too. Can you hold on to him?"

"Sure," he informed manfully, keeping his attention on the fishing line just as his grandfather had probably instructed him. Nevertheless, Chandra was ready to assist, no matter what they discovered dangling from the hook. Her help was finally needed when the fish had been reeled close to the dock. In the end, they worked together to scoop a large brassy brown fish from the lake.

Chandra looked down at the soaked front of her T-shirt and the rivulets of water dripping down her bare legs. Matt's clothes were in a similar condition since the fish had put up quite a struggle. Seeing the pride on the child's face, Chandra knew she would have jumped in the lake to net that fish if necessary. "Looks like you caught a seven, maybe eight-pound walleye," she judged incredulously.

With a solemn expression, Matt studied his catch. "It's a keeper, all right." Then he let out a whoop and the excitement of the moment overwhelmed his reserve. "Yippee! Mine's the biggest! Mine's the biggest!"

All dignity was thrown aside as Matt and Chandra did a victory dance on the dock until the weathered old boards were shaking. Unable to resist, she scooped Matt up, gave him a big hug and whirled him around and around. The exuberant giggles she'd longed to hear spilled like enchanted bubbles from his mouth.

Standing on the landing, Linc looked down at the woman and small child cavorting around on the dock. A huge lump developed in his throat as Matt's laughter echoed through the trees. Uninhibited, filled with joy, it was a sound that was far too rare. Somehow Chandra, a woman he didn't think would have the slightest interest in children, had found the key to Matt's heart. He was hugging her as tightly as he did the most dearly loved of his stuffed menagerie.

Linc leaned back against the landing rail and savored the sight. Chandra's hair was a mess. Her clothes were old, faded and wet. She was even barefoot. When Matt reached up with both hands and tousled her hair even more, she merely laughed and returned the favor. If Linc could believe his own eyes, there was far more to her than the glossy facade she displayed at the office.

He started walking down the hill, his grin growing wider and wider. Matt was obviously enjoying his position in Chandra's arms. He gave the little guy credit for holding on to a good thing. He knew from personal experience that Chandra was soft, warm—all in all, extremely huggable.

Exhausted, Chandra took Matt with her as she fell to her knees in a heap of giggles. She was delighted with his response to her affection. He felt so good in her arms. She couldn't resist hugging him tighter.

"Is this a private celebration or can I join you?" A deep voice rumbled from several feet above them.

"Uncle Linc! Look." Matt jumped up from Chandra's lap. Running to the net, he dragged it across the dock. "Me and Chandra caught a big ol' walleye!"

"You sure did, Matt," Linc complimented with a broad grin but kept his attention on the woman still sprawled on the dock. From Chandra's vantage point, he seemed to tower toward the sky. His legs were spread apart and looked as long and powerful beneath his faded jeans as two mighty tree trunks, but with far more interesting lines. His hands rested on his narrow hips and his broad chest, beneath a snug T-shirt, revealed its powerful musculature with each laughing breath he took.

Suddenly aware of her disheveled appearance, Chandra pushed her tumbled hair away from her face and attempted to smooth it. She imagined she must look as if she'd stuck her finger in an electrical outlet and wished she'd brought along a scarf, a bandanna, hat—anything to disguise the unruly mass of curls. As she moved to get to her feet, Linc offered his hand. She stared at it warily for a moment, recalling what had happened the last time he'd offered her assistance.

Knowing it would be churlish to refuse his help, she placed her hand in his. He pulled her up so rapidly, she continued the motion until she rammed into his chest. His arms went around her to steady her and hers automatically wrapped around his trim middle. Chest to chest, thigh to thigh, their startled gazes met and awareness of their natural and exciting physical differences shafted through Chandra's body as strongly as it had the night before.

Her soft breasts fitted against the rigid planes of his chest and her entire body felt tight. The reaction was most obvious in her nipples, which instantly hardened into points beneath the softness of her damp T-shirt and bra. Her smooth thighs, bare beneath the ragged hem of her cutoffs, recorded every nuance and fiber of the surface of Linc's jeans. The smooth pliancy of worn denim and the unyielding cords of masculine muscles pushed at the fabric from the inside. All these details were documented in the split second before they moved apart.

Unfortunately, as Chandra backed away her bare foot came down squarely on the fish. Her startled cry shattered the tension between them.

The shock of something cold and scaly squirming beneath the sensitive skin of her arch sent Chandra pitching forward again into the security of Linc's arms. "You really have trouble staying on your feet around me, don't you?" he asked.

Feeling ridiculous to the extreme, she wriggled within his arms, trying to escape. However, Linc merely laughed and tightened his grasp, increasing her nervousness.

Unreasonably, Chandra blamed him for her hysterical reaction. If he hadn't raised all of her nerves to the peak of their sensitivity, she wouldn't have behaved so idiotically. If he hadn't been there, she would have had her wits about her and not backed right up on Matt's prize catch.

"It's not funny," she muttered defensively, finally having some success pushing out of Linc's arms but carefully looking backward first to make sure of her footing. "I almost ruined Matt's fish."

"You're not heavy enough to smash that monster," Linc deemed with a wide grin, covering his disappointment that she had moved away.

He'd allowed himself the luxury of holding her soft curves against him far longer than was necessary but she'd felt so good. If Henry and the boys hadn't been there he knew he would have done far more than hold her. As it was he'd had a lot of difficulty keeping his hands from slipping below her waist and fitting her tightly against him. No matter how many times he told himself he shouldn't succumb to his desire for her, whenever he saw her all caution slipped away. The need to touch her was rapidly becoming more important than anything else.

If he hadn't left so quickly this morning he would have given in to the reactions his body had experienced at the sight of her sleep-softened mouth and the shower-fresh scent of her when she'd greeted him at the door in nothing but a bathrobe. As it was, all day he'd thought of little else. With each stroke of his paintbrush as he'd applied the final coat of stain to his front porch, he'd thought of what it would be like to stroke her body.

It was stupid, he'd told himself. He couldn't get involved with her. He'd half hoped that the next time he ran into her his crazy infatuation would have disappeared. It hadn't. If anything it was more intense than ever and he was going to have to find a way to rid himself of this craving he had for her or swiftly go insane.

When he'd arrived, looking for Henry and the boys, he certainly hadn't expected to find Chandra on the dock wrestling in joyful abandon with Matt. Nor had he expected to react so powerfully when she'd fallen into his arms. He'd thought he had some willpower to resist the desire she aroused in him every time she turned those soft brown eyes in his direction. He was dead wrong.

Henry, Ted and Chas paddled to the shore and beached their canoe. Ted proudly held up their string of fish while everyone applauded Matt's angling prowess with appropriate enthusiasm. "We're through fishing, let's go swimming," Chas shouted, his tennis shoes already off his feet and his fingers at the hem of his shirt. His brothers quickly followed suit.

"Hold on, guys!" Linc shouted, bringing them all to a halt. "Your trunks are still at home."

Puzzlement knitting his brows, Chas tilted his head to one side and queried, "So what? We never used them here before."

"There's a lady present," Linc reminded, and Chandra was immediately the target of three pairs of disappointed brown eyes.

"I'll go on up to the house and you can have your swim," Chandra suggested, rewarded by the return of the boys' smiles. "I'll send some towels down with Henry," she offered as she started her retreat. "Next time bring your suits, and I'll swim with you." *You're pushing yourself on them again!* she reprimanded herself before stammering, "Ah. . .I mean if you'll let me."

"You can swim this time too," Matt invited, not having understood why her presence should have prevented their swim in the first place. Hearing his brothers' snickers behind his back, he rounded on them. "Chandra said the lake is for everybody, even her!"

"How about it?" Linc inserted, a challenging light in his azure eyes. "You want to go skinny-dipping with us, Chandra? We won't mind if you don't."

It was a dare and she knew it. She also knew Linc didn't expect her to accept it. However, if three little boys and their grandfather hadn't been present, Chandra would have gladly taken up the challenge if for no other reason than to show Lincoln Young she was no prissy city woman. This was not the appropriate time or activity to prove that to him so she backed down.

Sending him a glacial look, Chandra said, "I think I'll pass." Lest he'd missed the meaning of her glare, she added for good measure, "At least this time— Uncle Linc."

7

Boisterous laughter and squeals resounded through the trees and it was all Chandra could do not to sneak a peek at Linc and the boys romping in the lake. "It sounds like they're having a good time," she commented across the picnic table to Henry. "Linc seems like a good father."

Henry looked up from cleaning fish and smiled. "He knows how to play. He has brought back the laughter to my grandsons. They have lost much but also have found much. Linc has provided a stability that would not have been theirs had my son lived. Joe loved his children but was tied to the wind and could not stay in one place. Now the boys have a secure place to call their own and a father who will always be there for them."

Chandra's eyes widened with surprise. "Has Linc adopted the boys?"

"He has adopted them in his heart," Henry explained. "But there will be no papers to prove it. He wants them to remember who they are and be proud they carry the Raincloud name. He will not let them forget they have sprung from the Chippewa nation." Wistfully, he added, "In the world Joe chose, that was difficult."

Chandra would have liked to learn more but heard

Linc telling the boys it was time for them to get out of the water. Swiftly she finished cleaning the last sunfish and tossed it into the pan with the others. "That's it," she announced. With fascination she watched Henry's deft movements as he quickly turned Matt's walleye into serving-size fillets.

"I'll go in the house and start the rest of the meal. I'm sure I can leave all the fire-building and grilling to you." She wiped her hands on a rag and turned toward the house. "There's a bag of charcoal and some lighter fluid in the shed . . . unless that's beneath you," she teased.

"I will use it," Henry replied. "We Chippewa are a practical people. The Great Spirit gave us the fire long, long ago." A smile tugged at the corners of his wide mouth and merriment twinkled from his dark eyes. "He also told us to feed our bellies when we are hungry. My belly is calling out to me with an urgent voice. The charcoal and lighter will make the rumbling stop sooner."

"I think so too," Chandra agreed with a small laugh, her own eyes reflecting Henry's merriment. "You Chippewa aren't the only practical people. Why do you think I wanted to go fishing with you? I knew darn well I wouldn't be able to catch a decent dinner all by myself after all that rain."

Henry's responding laughter followed her into the house. Once inside Chandra quickly went to work, gathering the ingredients for the rest of the meal. As she pulled out a sack of frozen french fries from her freezer and flipped on the oven to preheat it, some of her enjoyment fled. She'd persuaded Henry to stay for dinner with no trouble, now all she had to do was persuade Linc and the boys.

She was pretty sure Matt would accept the invitation, as they'd become friends during their afternoon sitting on the dock, but the other boys and Linc? Looking around the kitchen, she spied the cherry pie she'd baked earlier, glad now that she'd turned her early-morning frustration into a baking spree before lethargy had set in. At the time she'd wondered what she would do with a large pie and two dozen cookies and had anticipated either going on an eating binge or freezing everything but the pie.

The cookies had disappeared after she'd shamelessly offered them as a bribe—wouldn't the pie be just as effective? If the way to a man's heart was through his stomach, then she needed all the baked goods she could create. She had four men's hearts to conquer. That thought made her nearly drop the head of cabbage she was vigorously shredding for coleslaw. Was that what she wanted? Was she trying to win over the children in the hope that their uncle would follow suit?

When she'd issued the invitation to Henry to stay for dinner, it had seemed the logical ending to the day. Now, she realized it had been prompted by more than logic or even her own dislike of eating alone. She wanted to get to know the boys better and find out a whole lot more about their relationship with Linc. Also, little Matthew's huge black eyes and angelic face pulled at her heart and brought motherly instincts to the surface that she'd submerged beneath her career-woman facade for far too long.

More and more, recently, she'd thought about having a family and realized that she'd better do something soon before her time ran out. She certain-

ly wasn't planning on jumping into marriage merely
to indulge her maternal instincts, but she was admit-
tedly more open to such a commitment than she'd
ever been before. Was it because she'd come back to
the cabin, filled with the memories of her parents
who'd been so happily married and seemed so delighted to have a child? Was she trying to recreate for
herself some of that happiness she'd viewed strictly
through a child's eyes? Had her parents' life together
really been what she'd thought?

Watch it, Chandra. Lincoln Young turned you on
before you knew he was the solo parent of three little
boys. Given your present state of mind, you'll be try-
ing to drag him off to the nearest preacher as soon as
supper is over. There was a lot more to think about
here than satisfying her own biological urges, beginning with the fact that Linc appeared to lust after her
body but wanted no commitments. To be honest, she
wasn't sure that her attraction to Linc was based on
anything more than physical desire and the sentimen-
tal yearnings she had experienced since coming back
to the cabin.

"Thanks for the use of the towels." The central figure in Chandra's thoughts strolled through the back
door, carrying a bundle of wet towels in one hand
and his T-shirt in the other. "I'll take these home and
launder them for you."

"That won't be necessary," Chandra mumbled as
she stared spellbound at Linc's bare chest, still damp
from his swim. Confronted with that wide expanse of
heavy muscles covered with gold-tipped curling hair,
she was having trouble swallowing. She couldn't prevent the naked image of the rest of him from re-

turning to her mind, making it difficult to breath.

"Look, I've got a washer and dryer and we do laundry nearly every day. I'll have them back to you by tomorrow," he continued as if oblivious of the effect he was having on her. "Thanks for everything. We'll be going now."

Chandra stood immobile until the meaning of his words sifted through the utterly lascivious thoughts she was having. Linc was nearly through the door before she called out. "No! You can't leave yet. Didn't Henry tell you I invited everyone to stay for dinner?"

Disbelief was evident in the openmouthed look he gave her. "No, he didn't. It's very nice of you to invite us," Linc said politely. "But we've already taken up most of your day and we don't want to put you to so much trouble."

"It's no trouble, really. The boys have provided the main course and everything else is almost ready." *The pie, don't forget the pie!* Pointing to the lattice-topped pastry on the counter she said, "I went on a baking binge this morning and I can't eat that all by myself. Please, I'd like for you, Henry and the boys to stay for dinner."

Linc still didn't look receptive to the idea and kept one hand on the screen door. Chandra was more determined than ever to override his refusal, no matter how politely he had worded it. If he was worried about where the attraction between them might lead, he needn't worry tonight. They'd be more than adequately chaperoned during the meal. What happened later was up to him and they would deal with it when the time came.

Placing her hands on her hips, she threatened with a mock frown, "If you don't, I'll hold you directly responsible for the weight I'll gain this weekend." He was already responsible for her having baked all those goodies. The least he could do was save her from stuffing them in her own mouth.

Her nonsensical threat stopped him. He stepped back into the kitchen and plopped the sodden towels on the counter. Chandra wasn't sure if she was glad or disappointed when he pulled his shirt on, but she did sense that he was weakening.

To insure the victory, she stated in a no-nonsense tone, "There are three hungry little boys out there who can be satisfied in less than a half hour if you all stay. What were you planning for dinner?"

Linc leaned back against the counter, folding his arms across his chest and began close study of her. "What was I planning?"

He repeated her question but Chandra sensed he wasn't thinking of his menu for the evening meal. She was also aware that his intense perusal covered every inch of her but she grew most uncomfortable when his gaze centered on her face, as if searching for something.

Evidently satisfied with what he found there, he grinned. "Okay, lady, you got me. Whatever I could have come up with to accompany those fish couldn't compete with homemade cherry pie."

"It's about time you saw the merit in this," Chandra said with an approving smile. "For a man who works with figures all the time, you don't always operate logically. Now that that's settled, carry these things out to the picnic table but remember to spread this out first." She tossed a plastic tablecloth to him.

"Oh, I operate logically." Linc argued, tucking the tablecloth beneath his arm and accepting the stack of paper plates she handed him. The meaning of that statement missed Chandra but his next one didn't.

Blatantly staring at her hips and then her breasts, he remarked, "I do understand figures, and yours wouldn't have suffered overmuch from eating the pie all by yourself. It could stand some credits. If you have any more debits, you'll almost be operating at a loss."

"TALKING CURLS, HUH?" Linc teased. "Seems like Stumbling Curls might be more appropriate."

"Listen here, buster. This pie can be cut in five pieces just as easily as six," Chandra retorted in a mock-threatening tone. Her knife hovered over the pie while she fixed him with an affronted glare. It was difficult to maintain a straight face against the mischievous light in Linc's eyes and the wide grin on his face.

"Indian names are chosen to describe first impressions of a child," Henry intervened, coming to Chandra's defense. "Sometimes the name reflects the true character of the person or what the parent hopes it will be."

"What did you name Linc?" Chandra asked, hoping there would be something about his Indian name that would give her the ammunition necessary to turn the tables.

"Gold Spear," Henry supplied.

"Gold Spear?" Chandra hooted, directing her

laughing incredulity at Linc. Linc merely shrugged but brushed his hand across his mouth as if erasing a smirk.

"It fits him, for he is golden of head and walks tall and straight," Henry supplied, either oblivious to Chandra's hilarity or choosing to ignore it.

Linc threw her a grin, his superior stance fortified by Henry's glowing estimation of him. Throwing caution to the wind, Chandra risked bringing up a reference to the night before. If he could tease her about falling into his arms that afternoon when it had been entirely as much an accident as the previous night's tumble to the floor, she could do the same.

"Walks tall and straight, eh?" Chandra mimicked Linc's mocking manner. It seemed the perfect time to use humor to soften the effects of last night, especially with Henry and the boys in attendance to provide a buffer. Maybe then the humiliating memory could be put aside.

Chandra directed her statement at Linc, hoping to erase some of his cockiness but not the relaxed camaraderie that had developed between them during the meal. "Something tells me even Gold Spear can lose his balance and take a header."

"But Gold Spear chooses his landing spots wisely," Linc supplied smoothly.

Not to be outdone, Chandra grumbled, "The spot might claim otherwise."

"Ah, but Gold Spear found the spot very soft and most receptive to his thrust," he returned, a dazzling light shafting from his eyes and enveloping her in its warmth.

Horrified, Chandra glanced at Henry but he was

speaking to Chas and appeared not to have heard Linc's suggestive remark. Extremely uneasy with the turn in the conversation, Chandra encompassed everyone when she asked, "Anyone want ice cream with their pie?"

A chorus of assent responded to her query and provided her with the chance to retreat graciously into the house. Once inside, Chandra leaned against the refrigerator, needing the soothing effect of the cold, smooth enamel against her heated brow. She was sorry now that she'd brought up any small reference to the night before. It certainly hadn't caused Linc any discomfort, while her embarrassment had intensified. The man seemed able to turn his emotions on and off as easily as a water spigot and with as little effort!

Knowing she couldn't cower in the kitchen forever, Chandra extracted the half gallon of ice cream from her freezer and a scoop from the drawer. Hearing the sound of Linc's laughter as he responded to something Matt had said, she wondered if her assessment of his emotional control was correct. She'd seen the way he interacted with the boys, sensed the way he felt about them and they toward him.

A person would have to be blind and totally insensitive not to see the love that was shared between Linc and the boys. Children needed constancy and unqualified love to be as secure as the Raincloud children and somehow Linc had provided it. He obviously restricted his on-and-off switches for her.

The cherry pie served à la mode proved a big success and even the reticent Ted complimented Chandra. Putting down the platter she was clearing from the table, Chandra gave his shoulder a light squeeze. "Thank you, Head in Clouds. I'm very glad you enjoyed it."

Ted graced Chandra with one of his rare smiles as if pleased she had remembered his Chippewa name. Henry had divulged everyone's Indian name while they polished off dessert. Reminding them of the old ways, he'd reminded them all not to use their names unless it was a very special occasion. He'd told them that a person never knew when bad spirits were listening and that they might remember the names and retaliate.

At this point the boys had begun looking over their shoulders, peering into the long shadows cast by the tall trees. Henry had waited in silence until he felt the proper reverence had been attained, then commented, "The strong medicine of your white mother will protect you from these spirits. As long as you remain good in your heart, they cannot harm you." After Henry's speech they had all felt free to use the lovely names he had chosen for them but not without some forethought.

"If you have a favorite dessert," Chandra informed Ted, "let me know and I'll try to make it for you. I enjoy baking and don't often have a good reason to do much of it." Tossing a playful jab at Linc, she added, "Laughing Squirrel says Uncle Linc isn't much of a baker."

Ted's smile faltered a little. "Sometimes Laughing Squirrel chatters too much."

"Hey, it's okay," Linc assured. "I'm the first to admit that my skills in the kitchen are limited."

"But you make real good hamburgers," Chas defended with all the fierceness that his Indian name, Little Bear, denoted.

"I asked Chandra to give you lessons," Matt revealed, his guileless expression hopeful. "Will you, Chandra?"

"Men don't take lessons from women," Ted maintained in true chauvinistic form. At the tender age of ten, he seemed to have taken much of the responsibility of his younger brothers onto his slender shoulders. So close to childhood but so wanting to be a man, he'd chosen to assert male supremacy as a means of establishing his position. Chandra understood but still felt a stab of disappointment.

Linc didn't miss the brief show of hurt that appeared on Chandra's face and then watched for a flair of anger, ready to buffer the situation if necessary. Instead of anger he saw understanding and realized he'd misjudged this woman once again. Still the situation between Ted and Chandra couldn't be left as it was, and he didn't believe Chandra knew how to counter Ted's accusation without hurting his sensitive feelings.

With a gentle tone that didn't threaten Ted's dignity, Linc corrected the boy. "Sometimes men can learn lessons from women. When a woman knows all about something, a man would be a fool not to ask for her help. Your teachers in school are women and you ask them for help, don't you?"

"Well..." Ted hedged, looking down at his feet. Gathering his courage, he looked up again at Chandra's face. "Some women are special, I guess."

"Thank you, Ted," Chandra said softly. "Some boys are very special too." The smile Ted sent her confirmed her interpretation of his remark, and she hoped she'd made a small advance toward winning his friendship.

"How about you and Chas helping me carry all this stuff in for Chandra?" Linc suggested. Seeing Chandra open her mouth to protest, he shook his head. "It's the least we can do to show our appreciation. Right, guys?"

Chas and Ted obediently set to work, though they didn't look too excited by the prospect. Nonetheless, Chandra was impressed; she'd disliked clearing the table when she was a child and guessed that the boys felt the same way about it. Even if they were on their best behavior because of her, Linc's handling of them was very effective. The boys were well behaved and respectful, a tribute to Linc's parenting.

Remembering how she had felt when her world had been turned upside down and the two people she'd loved the most had been killed, she could well imagine some of the problems Linc had faced. Chandra's aunt and uncle had weathered many a storm with her when she'd covered the hurt and pain of her loss with belligerence. There had been all too many times when she'd been obstinate, so filled with rage that her parents had been unfairly snatched away from her that she'd refused to respond to her aunt's entreaties. Unlike the boys, she had never established such a loving relationship with her guardians.

Settling herself back down on the bench next to Matt, she succumbed to the luxury of doing nothing but relaxing after the meal. She chatted quietly with Henry. He had taken out a piece of wood and sat whittling a small figure, a familiar sight from years past. After a few minutes, the quiet voices and full day of activity had their effect on Matt. He began yawning and blinking his eyes to remain awake.

Chandra slipped an arm around his shoulders and he seemed glad for the support, looking up with a smile as he snuggled closer.

"Do you have any little boys?" he asked.

"No, I don't, but I'd like to someday," Chandra answered honestly.

"What kind of boy would you like?"

"Chandra's resting, Matt," Linc spoke from the other side of the table. "Don't bother her with a lot of questions."

Chandra frowned but didn't say anything as Matt nestled more closely against her. Linc waited until he was sure the child was finished asking questions before picking up another load of dishes and going back to the kitchen. In the quiet that followed, Matt's yawns became more frequent and his small body seemed to be in danger of slipping off the bench. Automatically, Chandra lifted him onto her lap. By the time Linc and the other boys were finished clearing the picnic table and washing the dishes, Matt was sound asleep, his completely relaxed body snug and warm in Chandra's arms.

"I think it's time to get these guys home," Linc announced and reached for Matt. Chandra brushed her lips across Matt's tousled head before reluctantly relinquishing him, confused by the tight expression she saw on his uncle's face as he turned away.

Considering Chandra's unconscious behavior with Matt, Linc felt a renewal of the awareness that always lay just beyond his consciousness when he was near her. Quickly he stifled it. Spending a day with the boys, apparently enjoying it and even holding a sleeping child might be merely a novel experience to a woman like her. Even the affectionate caress she'd just given Matt probably didn't mean anything—did it? There was only one way to find out and the sooner the better.

If her behavior today was honest, then it might be possible for him to take a chance with her. God knows he wanted to. His feelings for her went beyond the physical but he had to find out if she felt the same way. He couldn't stand it if he let her have his heart and then found out she only wanted his body. Going in, she had to know that he and the boys came as part of a package. He didn't know if that was fair but he'd made his choice years before. If it came down to it, he'd have to choose them over her.

With Matt in his arms, Linc nodded to Chas and Ted. Both boys offered their thanks for the meal, then headed toward the truck. Linc settled Matt between his brothers on the front seat, then exchanged a few words with Henry.

Moments later, through the truck's window, he directed, "You two boys help your grandfather get the little guy into bed, okay? You can watch television for a while, then you go too. I have some things to do so don't wait up for me. I've persuaded your grandfather to spend the night, so don't give him any trouble or he might never do it again."

Since Henry preferred to stay in his own house, this was a rare treat. Ted and Chas eagerly agreed to be on their best behavior. Linc reached in and tousled their hair, then stepped back from the truck as Henry put it into gear.

Chandra leaned against one of the trees by the picnic table, watching the truck pull away, then saw Linc's long-legged figure turning back toward her. She expected him to mouth a quick goodbye, mount his cycle, then follow the truck but instead he walked right past it. *Don't set yourself up for another disappointment*, she warned inwardly at his approach. *He's probably just going to offer a few polite phrases and then be on his way.*

"We've probably cleaned you out of food but could you spare a cup of coffee?" Linc surprised her by asking.

"Uh. . .sure. I'd like one myself." Chandra heaved away from the tree.

Linc fell into step beside her, his hands tucked into the back pockets of his jeans. Looking up at the darkening sky, he remarked, "Still clear. Probably be a lot of stars out tonight."

"Probably," she agreed.

"Should be a nice day tomorrow."

"I hope so," she said but was totally confused by their inane conversation. She doubted very much that Linc had stayed behind to discuss the weather. Exactly what he wanted she wasn't sure but decided to be on her guard. "Will instant be all right with you?" she asked as they mounted the steps.

"What?"

"Instant coffee. Is that all right or would you prefer to wait for some to brew?" She gave him a puzzled look. He definitely had something on his mind and it wasn't a cup of coffee.

"Instant's fine. I don't want to put you to any trouble."

"It's no trouble." By now they had entered the kitchen and Chandra reached for the teakettle, uncomfortably aware of Linc's eyes on her. She turned on the burner beneath the kettle and busied herself spooning coffee crystals into two mugs, hoping Linc would say something. He didn't, just continued to watch her, studying her much too closely as if trying to delve beyond the surface of her skin. She wanted to scream, "What do you want?" but didn't.

"Actually I prefer instant," she finally said to break the silence.

"It's not bad," Linc agreed. "I don't like decaffeinated though."

"I've found some brands that are pretty good, but some do taste weak when you take out the caffeine." Egad, Chandra thought. If this kept up much longer, they'd either be discussing the merits of one brand of coffee over another or she'd have a nervous breakdown.

The teakettle whistled its readiness and Chandra poured the steaming water into the mugs. "Cream or sugar?"

"Black is fine."

Chandra plopped a sugar cube in hers and stirred it briskly. "Would you like to take these out on the deck? It's beautiful this time of the evening."

"Sounds good," he remarked and started toward the front of the cabin.

"It's getting a little chilly. I'll grab a sweater and join you in a minute." Whether the gooseflesh on her arms and legs was from the drop in temperature or the case of nerves she was developing, Chandra wasn't sure. In either event, she felt the need to more completely cover herself. Once in the bedroom, she hurriedly exchanged her cutoffs for a pair of corduroy slacks and the T-shirt for a fluffy sweater. Glancing at the mirror, she was horrified to see that she looked a fright.

"Probably why he's staring at you so strangely," she muttered under her breath as she pulled a brush through her curls and anchored them away from her face with a pair of tortoiseshell combs. Still not satisfied, she applied a touch of blusher and lip gloss, then a light spray of cologne. "At least I won't reek of fish anymore." She dropped the questionable-smelling T-shirt and raggedy shorts into the hamper on the way out of the bedroom.

Linc was leaning against the rails around the deck, his back to her, when Chandra stepped out the door. Her mug sat waiting on the railing near his elbow. He didn't turn when she joined him but continued to stare out across the lake. Chandra took a sip of coffee and decided she'd allow Linc one more minute of this silence before she demanded to know what was on his mind.

"Did you enjoy yourself today?" he asked, turning toward her and subjecting her to another of his steady perusals. Even in the dusky light she could see the intensity of his eyes, their blueness cutting through the space between them like a laser.

"Sure," she answered honestly. "That trio of yours is a lot of fun."

He moved his body slightly so that only one of his elbows rested on the railing. "You like children?"

"Yes I do," she returned, but her patience had fled. "What are you getting at? I wouldn't have invited myself to fish with the boys today nor would I have asked you all to stay for dinner if I didn't want their company. Why are you interrogating me?"

His stern expression softened and a touch of humor pulled at the corners of his mouth. Talking Curls was a good name for her; the thick mop of dark curls seemed to be just as accusing as the flash in her eyes and the tone of her voice. "Sorry, I guess I'm being paranoid. I suppose I was looking for an ulterior motive."

"What did you suppose I was doing?" Chandra demanded angrily. Once started she couldn't stop. "Pretending to enjoy your boys just to get to you?"

"It did cross my mind," Linc returned smoothly, not caring that his remark would increase Chandra's anger. He was deriving too much pleasure from watching her features change as her rage increased. The soft rosy mouth that drove him crazy pouted. In her anger her lips pursed into a tight little bud that unconsciously challenged him to kiss it open.

Before he could act on that impulse, Chandra sputtered, "Why of all the egotistical, conceited, vain...." The faintly amused smile he was giving her only added to her befuddled fury. "To think I actually thought you were shy when I first met you."

"Shy? You thought I was shy?" Unable to restrain himself any longer, Linc set down his coffee mug, took Chandra's from her startled hands and placed it beside his on the railing. Before she could offer another word, he pulled her into his arms and kissed her, not stopping until her rigid body relaxed against him. Still holding her imprisoned, he nibbled at the corners of her mouth. "Still think I'm shy?"

"Umm...no," Chandra managed, her senses reeling with the suddenness and thoroughness of his kiss. "Should've known better." His hands were running up and down her back, sending shivers through her body and making it difficult to form a coherent thought. "You're a lot of things but shy isn't one of them." She quivered as his lips nuzzled her lobe and his breath blew against the sensitive spot just behind her ear.

"What are all those things you think I am?" he asked as he pressed kisses along her jawline and down her throat. "Whatever they are, they won't compare with all the things I've thought about you."

8

"WE'VE ALREADY ESTABLISHED that you're an efficient accountant...." Chandra caught her breath when Linc's hands slipped below her waist and possessively cupped her bottom. "And one of the best...ah...financial officers I've ever encountered." Keep it light, she told herself. It was the only defense she had against the onslaught of his touch, scent, husky voice.

"Thank you," Linc murmured against her throat. "You're not bad yourself."

"I thought you said I needed some credits to my figure." Chandra pushed away from him, effectively stopping the kisses he was stringing along her throat. She didn't want to fall under the hypnotic spell of his eyes, didn't want to acquiesce to his teasing seduction as easily as she had the night before. Her pride wouldn't allow her to be cast in the role of aggressor again.

Through hooded eyes Linc gazed down at her, resting his palms over her hips. "What you have is all in the credit column. It just wouldn't hurt to pad your assets a little."

"You're impossible," she said with a nervous giggle and was immediately brought back into place by a firm hand on the middle of her back.

"Probably." He wrapped his arms tightly around her. "You feel so good." He breathed deeply. "And smell terrific." He buried his nose in her hair. "How can you smell so good after spending the day fishing?"

"Halston Night," she murmured, giving in to the desire to return his kisses by pressing her lips into his throat. "Covered up the fishy smell. And I got rid of the T-shirt."

"Aha!" Linc released her slightly, allowing a breath of space between them. "You wily woman. You are after me."

"I am not after—"

The rest of Chandra's denial was muffled by Linc's lips. Savoring her sweetness, he sipped at the bow of her mouth, ran his tongue along the outline, then pressed for entrance. She could no longer deny the currents that bolted between them. When he enfolded her more closely, she melted into him, fired by the sensations that sprinted through her as her soft body blended into the hard, virile contours of his. Chandra wrapped her arms around his waist and rising up on her toes, she returned his kiss.

Linc widened his stance, fitting her against the evidence of his desire. Thrilled by the feel of him, Chandra moaned softly from deep in her throat.

He tore his mouth away and gazed at her with an almost blinding intensity. "God help me, I need you. I need to make love to you," he breathed, his tone a mixture of anguish and resignation. Picking her up, he cradled her in his arms and started toward the door.

The fever that had burned away her reason abated

and Chandra returned to reality as Linc shifted her slightly in order to open the door. "Put me down, Linc."

Linc ignored her demand until they were inside the house. Then he slowly lowered her feet to the floor. He could feel the renewal of tension in her, sense the rejection that was building. He brushed a kiss across her forehead. "I want you, Chandra. Please say you want me." His hands curled around her waist and moved upward until his thumbs brushed against the undersides of her breasts.

Chandra caught his hands and moved them away. "Don't, Linc. Don't start this again. I'm the same woman I was last night. The same one you walked out on." She broke away from him and turned her back. Hugging herself, she shuddered. "I won't go through that again and I won't be made to feel as if all I'm after is a few minutes of pleasure. No matter what you may have thought, I don't indulge in meaningless passion."

"Last night was my fault, not yours," Linc offered guiltily, realizing how much his own fear had hurt her. He touched her shoulder, squeezing his eyes shut when she flinched. How could he possibly make her understand? "Chandra. Leaving you last night was the hardest thing I've ever done in my life but I had to. You scare the hell out of me, lady."

"Why?" Chandra protested. "Because you think you'll lose that good life you have if you become involved with me?" His hurtful parting words of the night before still stood as a barrier between them. She couldn't give in to the forces that drew her to him without losing her self-respect.

Not caring that she might be reminding him of a time and a person much better forgotten, she blurted defensively, "I don't know what happened between you and your wife but I don't want to have an affair with a man who's still carrying around some painful baggage from a past marriage."

Linc turned her around and tilted her chin up with his fingers. "My life with Jean has nothing to do with what's happening now. Whatever I felt for her died a long time ago. I don't know what Henry told you—"

"Henry didn't tell me anything. He didn't have to," Chandra insisted. "I'd have to be blind not to realize that you don't trust women. You desire me but you don't want to get involved. That's why you left me last night, isn't it? For some reason, every time we get close, I start reminding you of your ex-wife and you can't wait to get away from me."

"I'm not trying to get away from you now," he reminded her softly. "I've been divorced for three years, Chandra. It's part of my past, not my future. My concerns are all for you. Not many women want to get involved with a man who has three children. I have to be sure you know what you're getting into. I don't know where you and I are headed but I'm sure of one thing. I made a promise to Joe and I won't go back on it."

"Oh, Linc," Chandra vowed. "I'd never ask you to do that. I know what they mean to you and, more importantly, what you mean to them. I understand exactly how much children need someone to depend on, someone who accepts them for what they are. Please believe that I'd never try to take that away from them."

She could almost see his mind working as he analyzed her words. She was saddened by the painful struggle she could see in his eyes. He had to have been hurt very badly to be so hesitant. When he finally did speak, she would have done anything to alleviate the agony in his tone.

"I don't want to hurt you. It's been years since I've felt this way with a woman. Maybe I'm crazy for wanting you this badly but I can't stay away from you any longer. We might not be able to count on the future but we've got today."

"That's all anyone has," Chandra murmured. "I do want you, Linc. I want you tonight."

"You've got me." His strong mouth descended and took possession of hers again and again. There was something between them that was so volatile it needed only the slightest catalyst to explode into flames. The need to become one with him overrode everything else and Chandra stopped thinking.

Pressing against the heat of his body, Chandra gave in to the pleasure. Her tongue joined his in an ardent dance of erotic rhythm. Her breath quickened and the edges of consciousness blurred when he cupped her face between his palms and deepened the penetration of his kisses. Chandra's knees were shaking when he finally released her mouth. Her head fell limply against his chest and her hands groped for support at his shoulders.

"Not here," Linc muttered, sweeping his hands down her throat, lingering on her breasts as he steadied her.

Chandra took a deep breath, knowing that there was no turning back. She took one unsteady step toward the stairs leading to the loft before Linc picked her up in his arms again.

"Like I said—Stumbling Curls." He chuckled into her hair. "You'll never make it up those steps but we're not going to end up on the floor tonight. I want everything to be right."

With a sure step, Linc carried her up the stairs. Still holding her, he brushed the pile of pillows that served as a headboard onto the floor. Pulling back the down comforter, he lowered her onto the smooth sheets, then lay beside her.

Despite his consuming desire to feel her body beneath his, Linc warned himself to be careful with her. She wasn't really a tiny woman, just fragile and certainly much smaller than he, and he wanted to protect her.

They lay facing each other on the bed, hands touching lightly, skimming over the outlines of their bodies. "You're all soft, fluffy textures," Linc remarked as he grazed one palm up from the curve of her corduroy-covered hip and caught a handful of her sweater.

He pushed her gently onto her back and buried his face in the curve of her shoulder and neck. "It's so soft." His hand slid up under the downy angora to caress her rib cage. "But not as soft as what's underneath."

Chandra's hands were just as busy as she tugged his T-shirt free from his jeans and buried her fingertips in the curling down that surrounded his navel. She was thrilled by the sudden catch in his breath. "Oh, Linc, I've never wanted to touch and be touched like this." She skimmed her palms along his ribs, then over his muscled chest.

His shirt and her sweater were tossed to the floor, followed instantly by her bra. Their lips followed the paths forged by their hands. Chandra flicked her tongue across the peaks of his nipples while Linc teased hers with his fingers. The action was reversed and Chandra cried out with pleasure when he pulled one aroused bud beyond his lips, pressed it between his tongue and the roof of his mouth and stroked.

Her fingers plunged into his hair and pulled his head closer while her body arched upward, seeking greater intimacy. Sweeping her other hand down his back, she dipped her fingertips beneath the waistband of his jeans. "Oh yes," Linc whispered. "Help me out of these."

He raised his hips above her and Chandra released the snap and zipper of his jeans, gasping when her knuckles brushed against his hair-covered groin. He wasn't wearing any briefs. Freed of restrictions, the heated fullness of his maleness surged into her hand.

"Hold me," he said raggedly, half plea, half command, as he pushed himself into her warm palm.

Chandra's fingers closed around him, obeying his urgent directive. Somehow he shimmied out of his jeans while she started a sweet torture of bold, forceful caresses. Linc made short work of getting her out of the rest of her clothing, then hungrily took her mouth again.

While his tongue invaded, explored and conquered every crevice of her mouth, his hand swept down her torso, rotated on her silken belly, then moved lower. Linc sought and found the moist warmth of her, then teased the center of her pleasure until she yearned for fulfillment. "Now, Linc. Please, now," Chandra pleaded, reaching for him and guiding him toward the flowering portal of her body.

"Yes, sweetheart. Take me inside you."

He moved between her legs, lifted her upward and surged forward. Sheathed deeply within her, he heard her startled cry and condemned himself for hurting her. Beads of perspiration formed on his face and his body shuddered for release but he forced himself to gain control and withdraw.

"No," she managed breathlessly. Grasping his buttocks, inviting the thrusts Linc was trying so desperately to control, she urged, "Don't stop. Please don't stop."

"Chandra." Her name was a tormented moan torn from his throat as his constraint broke. A crescendo mounted into a driving rhythm that quickly hurled them both into a whirlwind of sensation. At the moment of that final vortex, they opened their eyes to drink in the sweeping emotion reflected in the other's face. Simultaneously, they cried out each other's name but the sound was swallowed as they joined their mouths at that highest peak of intimacy.

Chandra's eyes were moist as the tumult began to fade, replaced by a boneless languor. Linc lay heavily across her, his weight a satisfying pleasure. She sighed his name and brushed her hands listlessly across his glistening back.

Abruptly, Linc heaved himself up and away. Leaning over her, his expression was one of concern rather than the satisfaction she wanted to see. "I'm sorry. I didn't want to hurt you. I couldn't—"

"Shh," she ordered softly as she placed her fingers over his mouth. "You didn't hurt me. Far from it," she admitted, a gentle smile widening her lips.

"You're sure?" he queried, still not satisfied. "When you cried out, I ...." With his thumb, he caught a drop of moisture as it spilled from the corner of her eye.

"I've just never felt so...so...." She couldn't think of any single word that could possibly describe what she'd experienced at the moment of his possession. The quality of oneness had been so intense. She'd known Linc for barely a week and yet felt as if she'd been waiting for their union all of her life.

"Nor have I," he admitted, the concern etching his features into taut lines fading. His gaze softened and the corners of his mouth turned up into a satisfied grin. He dropped a brief kiss to her nose.

Grabbing up one of the pillows he'd tossed on the floor he tucked it beneath his head. After pulling up the comforter to cover them both, he settled Chandra along his side and nudged her head onto his shoulder. "Sweetheart, that was an extra-credit experience."

"You make it sound like some sort of test," Chandra said drowsily, nestling closer to his inviting warmth.

"No test. I'd already guessed you'd pass."

"Pass? I didn't know I was going to be graded!" Suddenly wide awake, Chandra struggled to sit up but Linc's arms tightened around her.

"Don't move," he growled, bringing her down across his body. Her breasts flattened against his chest and one of her thighs landed between his. "Mmm." He swept his hands down her back. "On second thought, I'm glad you moved. This is even better."

In mock anger, Chandra gibed, "More extra points?"

Capturing her head between his palms, Linc brought her face close to his. "You can't earn any more points in this area," he muttered before kissing her lightly. "You got 'em all." His lips covered her mouth, silencing further rebellion.

CHANDRA AWOKE TO AN EMPTY BED but the roar of a motorcycle signaled Lincoln's presence nearby. She glanced at the clock and saw that, just like the first time he'd interrupted her sleep, it was very early. Circumstances had certainly changed; this time, she wasn't the least bit irritated. In fact she intended to join him when he finished his ride and stripped off his leathers.

She hadn't been able to swim naked with him yesterday, but that was before he'd made love to her all night. Now, any and all of her misgivings about having a physical relationship with him had been thoroughly vanquished. She felt desired and cherished, filled with a joyful lightheartedness and hope for the future.

After last night, she knew that she was irrevocably in love with Linc. From the way he'd made love to her, she was sure he felt the same way about her. Neither one of them had been prepared for how swiftly the emotion had come upon them. It had just happened and now it was too late for doubts.

The possibility of anyone else being on her property this early was remote so Chandra didn't worry about walking outside in nothing but a knee-length, pink nylon robe. She was too impatient to issue Linc an invitation that he couldn't possibly refuse. When she reached the bottom step of the deck stairs, she stopped to listen and heard his motorcycle churning up sand on the beach at the foot of the hill. She hurried down the steep path.

It was a beautiful morning, the sun rising pink in the sky. White plumes of mist rose from the lake, looking like gold-sparkled gauze as they caught the dawning rays. Alongside the path, an abundance of ferns fanned the light, gentle breezes. Glistening dew shimmered on the emerald needles of the lofty firs and fell in brilliant showers as Chandra ducked under the low branches.

Upon reaching the earthwork landing, she located Linc on the granite shelf over the cove. A sickening feeling of déjà vu came over her. He was making that dangerous jump again! She didn't dare break his concentration as he prepared to launch himself and his bike over the water, but her anxiety built higher and higher as the ominous growl of the engine intensified.

She forced herself to keep her eyes open as bike and rider sailed through the air. Amazed that she was able to think at all, she noticed that he landed in exactly the same spot as he had the last time. She could still see the grooves left in the ground from his previous jump. For some reason, that made her feel better. It was as if he had calculated the jump down to the last centimeter. With the right speed and thrust, it appeared that Linc was able to duplicate the precise landing every time. Maybe it wasn't nearly as dangerous as it looked.

Linc was as pleased with himself as he had been the last time. He didn't compliment himself out loud or

raise a victorious fist to the sky, but when he pulled off
his helmet he was grinning from ear to ear. Chandra
felt a rising excitement as he swung his leg over the seat
and sauntered toward the water's edge. He looked incredibly sexy and Chandra experienced a resurgence
of desire—a desire that should have been thoroughly
satisfied after the night she'd just shared with him!

The tight brown leather hugged the sleek powerful
lines of his body, emphasizing every plane, bulge and
curve. The knee-high boots brought attention to his
long muscular legs and his masculine stride. Hands
on hips, feet spread apart, he stared out over the
lake, looking like a man who owned the world.
Chandra couldn't wait to get her hands on him.

"Did you deliberately go riding this morning to entice me out of bed?" she inquired softly, waiting for
him to turn around before she completed her descent
to the beach.

"By the looks of it, I'm the enticee not the enticer,"
Linc stated on a choked breath. "I can see right
through that skimpy pink thing you've got on."

"Oh dear!" Chandra proclaimed in mock embarrassment as she took another step down. "Perhaps I'd
better go. I wouldn't want you to think I'm a scarlet
woman."

"Too late," Linc growled, his blue eyes devouring
her slender curves. "I know a sultry temptress when I
see one." As if terrified by the provocative smolder in
her gaze, he held up both hands and began backing
away. "I have a feeling my virtue is in grave danger."

"Not at all," Chandra assured, swinging her hips as
she stalked him. "I'm simply here to conduct a survey."

"What kind of survey?" he asked suspiciously.

Chandra tried not to giggle when Lincoln finally realized he'd backed into the water and his expensive boots were getting wet. Scowling, he jumped forward to find her standing right in front of him, barring his escape. She reached out and slowly began pulling down the front zipper of his jacket. "I'm trying to find out all I can about zippers. Fascinating invention."

"Are you sure this is on the level, lady?" Linc inquired skeptically as she separated his jacket and slid her fingers inside the leather. He could see the pleasure in her eyes as she discovered he wore nothing underneath. "I've answered lots of surveys on zippers but no one's ever needed a hands-on inspection to gather their information before," he managed hoarsely as her soft, warm palms grazed his nipples with light, arousing strokes.

"I try to be more thorough than the average pollster," Chandra informed, smiling serenely as her fingers followed the line of golden hair that arrowed down his chest to the waistband of his tight pants.

"Most admirable. I apologize for thinking you might be trying to take advantage of me," Linc said in a husky tone that belied his supposed naiveté.

"Oops!" Chandra apologized as she undid the brass button on his pants. "That wasn't a zipper, was it?"

"Anyone could make an innocent mistake like that," Lincoln observed, sucking in his breath as he felt her grasp hold of the small tab below the button. A pulsing ache gathered force in his loins as she started pulling and he could feel the teeth of the steel zipper parting one by one. He wasn't going to be able to take much more of this and the woman who was providing such erotic torture was well aware of it.

"Now *this* is a zipper," Chandra declared triumphantly, her heart swelling as she noted the effect the downward movement of her hand was having on him. "And so is this." Her free hand found one of the side zippers and began a similar action.

A few moments later, Linc sat down on the beach to pull off his boots. His bare behind sank into the cold, wet sand but he hardly felt the discomfort. He had something far more urgent on his mind. "You are a sultry temptress." He tried to look incensed as he glanced up at the smiling woman who waited for him to complete undressing. "I never should have fallen for that survey routine."

Chandra nodded, her features taut with desire. "Next time, you'll know better."

"I hope not," Linc vowed fervently as he sprang to his feet. Fully aroused and intent on bringing this pleasurable seduction to a rapid conclusion, Linc pulled Chandra into his arms. The thin nylon of her robe rubbed against his already sensitized nerve endings and he swiftly sought the even more tantalizing feel of her satiny skin.

Chandra felt as if she had stopped breathing as Linc tugged on the single tie at her waist. In seconds she was naked, her throbbing breasts pressed against his chest, her buttocks cupped in his warm palms. "I hope not too," she whispered as the familiar flutters deep inside intensified to the point that she could barely remain standing.

Linc lowered his head and kissed her with all the

longing she felt for him. She wanted it to go on and
on, overwhelmed by the extreme pleasure his lips and
tongue gave to her. Every time he kissed her, he
seemed to stake a greater claim and that thought
made her dizzy. She felt as though he wanted to
devour her, he couldn't seem to get enough of her.
His lips searched for and found the deepest recesses
of her feminine soul.

Chandra was aware that he had lifted her into his
arms but most of her concentration was centered on
giving him all that he sought. Eyes closed, she clung
to him, her fingers clasped tightly around his neck.
She was completely enveloped in the smell and the
taste of him, the feel of his bare flesh against hers. He
was all heat, a surging, flaming heat that fused her to
him like a living brand.

She barely felt it when he laid her down upon a
dew-drenched bed of ferns. Opening her eyes, she
saw his head outlined by the sun, his hair glinting
gold in the light. To her, he was the perfect sun god
she had seen that first morning.

Chandra's heated gaze was met by twin prisms of
blue desire. "I want to take you here, Chandra.
When I'm inside you, become a part of you, we'll
also be joined with the wind, the sky and the sun. Let
me show you a harmony that can never be captured
within the walls of a man-made house."

Chandra's body slowly adjusted to the feel of the
cool fronds beneath her but couldn't adjust to the
primitive look on Linc's face. The playful amusement, the fun-loving lights in his blue eyes were
gone, replaced by something so elemental it was both
frightening and exciting. He looked like a naked war-

rior, proud and strong as he waited for the acceptance of his mate.

"You once asked who was the real me," Linc pronounced softly, his voice one with the whispering waves upon the shore and the warm summer wind in the trees. "This is the real me, Chandra. Here, where I can feel the sun on my face and the breath of the earth on my skin. I am *shogonos*, a white man, but my family is kin to the earth, sky and water."

He pressed a soft kiss on the tender skin of her throat. "Henry told me long ago that a man's heart away from nature becomes hard. Experience taught me the truth in that. Now, I try to stay close so I won't forget. How akin to nature are you, Chandra?"

9

THEY LAY FACE TO FACE, their bodies touching, yearning for the feel of the other, yet separated by a distance of the mind. Chandra tried to decipher Linc's closed expression, distressed by the intensity of his hard gaze, the urgency that had been in his question, "How akin to nature are you?"

She sensed he was asking her something of far more import than the words implied. Instinctively, she knew that her answer would either bring them closer together or break them apart, perhaps permanently. "Henry gave me that same bit of advice when I was a little girl. Until you reminded me, I'd forgotten the wisdom in that philosophy."

She smiled gently as she recalled those long-ago summer days when she'd been such a free spirit. That young girl no longer existed, but the woman she'd become could still adapt to new things. "I've been too busy in the past few years, worrying about my career and building a nice secure world for myself to think about much else."

When she saw Linc's mouth tighten, she quickly went on. "I didn't even realize how much I had missed all this until I came back here again. You're right, Linc. There is an honesty, a simplicity and beauty in nature that can't be duplicated in other places, surely not in an office in the city. I really love being here with you." Lifting her chin, she searched his face with her dark eyes.

Linc stared back at her. There was an expectant stillness about him, a strange bleakness in his expression. Chandra was almost certain he wanted to express something entirely different from the words that came out but something inside him, something she didn't understand, stopped him. "You don't need to say anything more, Chandra. I can see it all in your eyes."

Because she sensed the effort it had taken him to restrain the passion she had aroused before he'd carried her away from the lake, Chandra was expecting his kiss to be almost brutal, impatient with male hunger. It wasn't, not at all.

His lips on hers were like a gentle spring rain, his touch light as a soft, warm breeze. He kissed her eyes, her throat, the small mole on her cheek. His fingers curved over her shoulders, stroking and smoothing her skin with his fingertips.

He was one with the elements and slowly, inexorably, he made her one with him. Each kiss was adoration, each tender caress an ardent devotion. Like barren ground that only needed the benign forces of nature to flourish, Chandra's heart blossomed inside her chest. With selfless generosity, Linc provided her with the air she needed to breathe, the rock-hard stability of his body, and finally, the raging, all-consuming fire that melded them into a single being.

Chandra's fingers clenched into his hair as she succumbed to the trenchant, sensual currents that made her tremble in his arms. Coupled together, they shared a unison of sensation with mutual, abandoned delight. Their shuddering movements of love became part of the motion of the trees swaying above them and their joyful cries of fulfillment echoed toward the endless blue skies.

Still joined with him, heart, soul and body in perfect harmony with his, Chandra kept her eyes closed and listened. It was as if she could hear the sun proclaiming pride in its handiwork as it showered gold on their glistening skin. The wind offered a rushing whisper to cool their fevered flesh and the silver leaves in the tall birch tress seemed to tinkle with approving laughter. The earth did have music for those who listened and Linc had reminded her to listen closely and well.

What he'd said before was true. They had just experienced a harmony that could never be achieved beneath the covers of a warm bed under a man-made roof. "I love you, Gold Spear," she whispered, her words encompassing the earth, the sky and the very special man who had just given her such a wondrous gift.

"And I you, Talking Curls," Linc whispered back, his smile dawning bright as the morning sun. "The spirits have been kind to send me a woman who gives me so much."

After leaving the fragrant bed of ferns, they cavorted about in the water like two carefree children. Chandra vowed to enroll herself in a YWCA swimming class as Linc swam circles around her, ducking her head beneath the water and laughing when she sputtered and floundered about. When she grew tired and sank like a stone, he would hold her up in the water until she'd regained her breath.

Often, after he was sure she was completely recovered, he would take possession of her mouth and draw her with him below the surface. There, in a silent world of feeling, he would caress the gooseflesh from her naked skin with warm languid hands until the inner heat was so intense she no longer felt the cold from the spring-fed water. Chandra wanted the idyllic interlude to last forever.

He made love to her once more on the beach before the fast-rising sun told them that it was time for him to go. The boys expected him to be home for breakfast and would worry if he wasn't there. Chandra was disappointed but understood that it was too soon and there was too much still unsettled between herself and Linc for her to be treated as part of the family.

She had known where Matt's questions the night before had been leading and she didn't want him counting on something that might not come to pass. Marriage had yet to be discussed. She and Linc had overcome a major hurdle but she knew they had many more to conquer before Linc was convinced that she had room in her heart for all five of them—Linc, Henry and the boys. Linc took his responsibilities seriously and she had to respect him for that. He had to be absolutely certain of her before he offered a permanent commitment.

"On weekends, I'm the cook," Linc informed her. "As they told you, I'm not very good but they seem to like my blueberry pancakes. If I don't hurry, they'll be beating down the bushes looking for me."

"It's still very early. Are you sure they're up already?" Chandra asked as she tightened the sash of her robe.

"If not, they will be soon. I wish I didn't have to but I've got to go."

While he got dressed, they made pleasant small talk. He mounted his motorcycle, then grabbed hold of her arm and pulled her up onto his lap. He gave her a tender kiss and set her gently back on her feet. "Like I said, I wish I could stay or at least come back later. Unfortunately, there's a festival at the reservation today and I promised the boys that I'd take them."

He curved his palm to her cheek. "You do understand, don't you?"

"Of course," Chandra reassured.

"Then I'll see you at work tomorrow," he said as he put on his helmet. "I'd offer to pick you up in the morning, but I've got a breakfast meeting downtown with Thad so I probably won't get to the office much before ten. Thad's going after a big contract and he needs me along to talk money."

"That's okay," Chandra said. "I need to be in early to supervise the inventory in the warehouse. The foreman said they would be starting at eight."

Linc nodded, then jumped down on the kick-start of his motorcycle. The noise from the engine brought an end to all conversation. He gave her a jaunty wave as he drove down the road and out of sight.

As she thoughtfully mounted the steps to the cabin, Chandra tried to tell herself that she shouldn't be disappointed at not being able to spend the day with him. After all, he probably didn't see much of the boys during the week. His place was with them right now, not with her. He was right not wanting to spring his relationship with her onto his family before they got to know her better.

She had to be patient and understanding. Passion had escalated into love very quickly for them but they were adults. It would take much more time for the boys to accept her into their home and their hearts. If she wanted to be part of Linc's family, she had to go slowly, earn the boys' friendship and trust before barging in on their lives.

Still, she wanted to spend every waking moment with him. She yearned to tell him everything he could possibly want to know about her but he hadn't posed a single, curious question or offered any new insights about himself. Maybe he had already learned all he wanted to know. She would make love with him whenever and wherever he chose.

DURING THE FOLLOWING WEEK, Chandra saw very little of Linc, though there was no way to prove that his reasons for being out of the office so often had any other basis than the one he gave. Thaddeus Hammond was trying to obtain a huge contract for Hammond Paper with a local packaging firm and Linc was handling the financial negotiations. When he did come into the office, he buried himself beneath stacks of paperwork.

He was pleasant and warm the few times he did talk to her, had even stolen a kiss or two when he was sure they were alone, but Chandra began having doubts about his feelings toward her. If he really loved her, wouldn't he try to make more time for her? Why did she feel like the last entry on his list of things to do?

He had stopped in at the cabin late Wednesday evening, and although he had kissed his way past her defenses, made love to her like a starving man, he hadn't been able to stay long enough to resolve anything else but the fact that they still desired each other. Chandra had wanted to state in no uncertain terms that they really needed to talk but Linc's obvious fatigue and his guilt over the short amount of time he'd been able to spend with the boys since the weekend had convinced her to postpone their discussion. Where he was concerned, Chandra discovered she was about as strong-willed and decisive as a soft wad of Silly Putty.

Thursday, after not seeing Linc all day, she decided to drive over to his house and get her feelings out in the open. Although the trim had yet to be stained and the cedar-board and batten siding wasn't completely up yet, the house was beautiful. Compared to Henry's one story cabin, Linc's home was immense. The three-tiered structure was designed to blend in with its natural surroundings and did nothing to take away from the rustic beauty of its setting.

After repeatedly banging with the shiny brass knocker attached to the thick oak door, Chandra realized that no one was home even though several lights were still on in the house. She'd noticed Henry's cabin had been completely dark as she'd driven by so she had no idea where everyone could have gone. After a few more minutes, she decided that her talk with Linc would have to wait for another day. He hadn't invited her over and obviously he and his family had made other plans for the evening.

On Friday, Linc didn't get into the office until well past noon. "If Collins and Taylor audits our firm next year," he stated without preamble as he strode around her desk and grasped hold of her arms, "you'll find we've doubled our profits. It took four days of nonstop meetings but Perry Packaging just signed on the dotted line."

Before Chandra could get anything out of her mouth but an uncaring, "That's nice," Linc had hauled her up out of her chair and sealed her lips with his own.

Linc could feel the resistance in her body but didn't understand the cause. He lifted his mouth and growled, "What's wrong, Chandra? I thought you'd be as hungry for this as I am."

"Sorry. You know what it's like to have so many things on your mind all at once," Chandra asserted, tension radiating from her body. "You may like to think so, Linc, but I haven't been sitting around like some adoring lapdog waiting for its beloved owner to come pet him."

Linc lifted a golden brow at her peevish tone. "I never thought that."

"Well, that's good because I've had far more urgent things filling up my agenda."

"More urgent than the need to kiss me? I've been looking forward to seeing you all day. I thought you'd feel the same way."

Determined to show him that she was every bit as involved with her work as he was with his, she made a sweeping gesture over her desk with her arm. "I do but I've got to get through all of those marketing figures before I meet with Bob Timmons this afternoon. He'll be out of town for the next two weeks so I've got to rush with his departmental workup and finish it before he leaves."

"Meaning work always comes first with you."

"I didn't say that," Chandra corrected. "But I have accepted this job and it's my responsibility to see that it's done right."

She was both annoyed and gratified by the disappointment she saw in his expression. Why did he think she should drop everything just because he'd found a few minutes to spare for her? On the other had, it did appear that he'd missed being with her, maybe even as much as she'd missed being with him.

"I was hoping we could spend the evening together," he stated, dropping her arms and stepping back. "But I'll understand if you can't make it."

He was clearly ready for her to tell him she was going to be busy for the entire evening. Chandra almost did exactly that until she noted the bitter disappointment gathering force in his taut features. "I should be home a little before seven." Not wanting to sound too anxious, she concluded flatly, "You can come over around seven-thirty if you feel like it."

It was as if a shutter came down over his face. Seeing it, Chandra was sure her deliberate attempt at indifference had hurt him. As petty as it was, she couldn't help but feel a surge of happiness. If she had the power to hurt him, he had to care for her quite a bit. "Should I expect you?" she asked with just the right amount of anticipation.

"The boys were hoping...." His voice trailed off

as he turned away to his own desk. "I suppose you'll be working over the weekend too?"

Chandra ignored the last and responded to the first. "The boys were hoping what?"

"I just wasn't thinking," Linc admitted dully. "I knew they were planning on this dinner and I stupidly assumed. . . ." He raked one hand through his hair, his features tight. "Oh hell, I told the little guys you'd come over to have dinner with us tonight and never issued the invitation. I got totally involved in that Perry deal and didn't even consider the possibility that you might get tied up with the audit."

He threw himself down in the chair, one hand savagely tugging loose his silk tie. "They're going to murder me and I deserve it. I can hear Henry now. He's been reminding me to invite you over all week. I just assumed you'd be available."

There was no double meaning to the statement and Linc looked so disgusted with himself that Chandra immediately forgave him for the neglect she had suffered at his hands. She forgave him, but didn't hasten to put him out of his misery. "What time was this dinner supposed to take place?"

"Six-thirty."

"I see." Chandra settled back down behind her desk and reached for the top paper on a tall stack. "Then I'd better get busy."

Almost a full minute went by before Linc asked, "Does that mean you're going to come?"

"I refuse to allow those boys to murder you," Chandra declared without looking up from the papers. "That's one pleasure I've reserved for myself."

After another long, speaking pause, Linc injected

in a guilt-ridden tone, "I've been taking an awful lot
for granted lately, haven't I?"

"Mmm," Chandra agreed.

"And for the past few days, I, not you, have put
work ahead of everything else."

"So it would seem," Chandra said, nodding, keeping her face down so he wouldn't see her smile.

"I forgot to listen for the music."

"Or else you heard a few sour notes and decided to
turn down the volume." Chandra looked him square
in the face, not bothering to hide the anxiety that fur-
rowed her smooth brow. "Are things happening too
quickly for you, Linc?"

"Things?" Linc returned, trying to ease her fears
with a light tone. "If by things you mean what's going on between us, then put your mind at rest. We've
already discovered what we want. Now all that's left
to do is see if we can live with it. I'm looking forward
to finding out."

To Chandra, that was not only a less than romantic description of their involvement but an awfully
cryptic forecast of the future. She needed clarifica-
tion. "Meaning we love each other and now we have
to decide what we're going to do about it?"

"Exactly," Linc agreed, then pointed to the papers
on her desk. "But first things first. You've got work
to do, lady."

THE FIRST THING CHANDRA SAW upon entering Linc's
kitchen was a huge poster taped to the refrigerator
door. "Hare and Hounds" was printed in bold black
letters over the picture of a man in a flaming red
jumpsuit, triumphantly riding a motorcycle across a

finish line. Chandra vividly remembered the day Linc had written those words in the sand. Now she understood that they referred to some kind of motorcycle race.

Noticing her interest, Chas ran over to the sign and pointed to the bike. "We'll be racing a better machine than that. That's a piece of junk. We've got a custom-built, 550cc dirt racer. Those suckers will eat our dust. Hell, we're gonna win that baby standing still. No sweat, Chandra."

Since Chas was only eight, Chandra suspected he was quoting a speech he'd heard from someone with a much more colorful vocabulary. She couldn't imagine from whom. She'd never heard Linc brag about his bike or his riding, at least not when he'd been aware of her presence and certainly not in such macho terms. She didn't think she approved of Chas's attitude toward the bike or the race.

"Are we now?" she asked sardonically, throwing a dark look over Chas's head to his guardian, who was busy directing traffic between the large butcher block that stood in the center of the floor and the trestle table. Evidently Linc hadn't heard a word of Chas's speech and didn't understand Chandra's glower.

"Something wrong?" Taking note of the bright glow in Chas's eyes and the enthusiastic expression on his face, Linc groaned, "Okay, pal. What have you been saying?"

Chandra was glad to see the guilty surge of color come up in the boy's cheeks as he attempted to sidestep the question by switching the subject. "Gee! I forgot to get the Jello-O, Uncle Linc." He pulled open the refrigerator door, ostensibly to correct the omission, but both adults who watched the maneuver were aware that it was a defensive ploy. "Here it is. I'll just take it to the table. Then we can eat before the food gets cold."

Chandra struggled to keep from smiling as Linc waited for Chas to pass by him before lifting the large bowl out of his hands and setting it down on the nearest counter. "Not so fast," he cautioned shortly as he reached down and picked Chas up off the floor. Plunking him down none too gently on the counter top, he continued his grilling. "How come I get the feeling you've been quoting from Danny Pelican again?"

Glancing over at Chandra, he informed her, "Danny's president of the Red Liners, an exclusive biking organization. Chas is too young to join but he thinks if he sounds like Danny, they'll make an exception in his case."

Chandra frowned, her concern growing. It sounded as if Chas was attracted to a very unsavory group. How on earth had someone so young been exposed to such an organization? Wasn't Linc aware of what his boys did after school? Whom they were with and where?

Before Chandra had a chance to voice another question, Ted entered the conversation. Giving his younger brother a condescending stare, he pronounced, "The Red Liners are dumb. Danny thinks he's so tough but he's all talk."

Linc flashed a stern warning with his eyes, and Ted quickly reached for a stack of paper napkins and hurried back across the kitchen. Linc continued his explanation to Chandra. "The esteemed Mr. Pelican is ten. He got an expensive bicycle for his birthday and spends most of his time showing off for the younger boys. He started a racing club composed of other boys his age. They meet on the school playground and see who can do the best wheelies."

"I see," Chandra said, her lips quirking as all her fears were put to rest. She had the grace to look a bit sheepish as Linc grinned at her, then turned back to the small boy seated on the counter.

"You know how I feel about that kind of talk, don't you, Chas?"

"Uh-huh," Chas mumbled, hanging his head.

"So why were you talking like that to Chandra?"

"I don't know," Chas tried, then saw that the answer wasn't going to get him off the hot seat. "I'm sorry." He lifted his chin.

Linc nodded, then admonished, "The race is for charity, Chas. The only real winner is going to be the Indian Culture Exchange. That's what you should be proud of, isn't it?"

"Yes, sir," Chas agreed. Suitably chastened, he was lifted down from the counter and allowed to join his brothers at the table.

During the meal, a tasty version of hunter's stew, Chandra learned all about the modified Hare and Hounds race that was scheduled to take place a week from Sunday. Customarily a hundred-mile chase over rugged terrain, this particular event was dirt racing over a fifty-mile, vaguely defined course. All proceeds from the gate would go toward funding an educational program intended to renew pride and confidence in the Indian heritage and give non-

Indians the opportunity to learn about the history of their Chippewa schoolmates.

Sponsored by an Indian Action Committee, the race provided an afternoon's enjoyment for the spectators and a respectable challenge to local amateur bikers, as well as the necessary dollars for the Culture Exchange. As Chandra continued to ask questions, she got the feeling that Linc was watching her closely, weighing every word that came out of her mouth as if searching for hidden meanings. When they were alone, she intended to find out why he seemed unable to accept her words at face value.

She didn't have to wait until they were alone. When the meal was concluded, she volunteered to help Ted and Chas with the dishes. Matt had almost fallen asleep in his stew and Linc had left the kitchen to put him to bed. Henry was excused from cleanup, since he had supervised all the cooking. Once again it was Chas who brought up a topic of conversation of which his guardian surely would not have approved. He began talking about the first few months after his parents had died, describing what it had been like to go and live with Linc and his wife Jean.

"You're nicer than her," he complimented, brown eyes wide and sincere. "She always said we were too noisy and made too much mess in her nice house. She didn't like stuff like fishing and motorcycles either."

Knowing she shouldn't allow him to continue, Chandra nevertheless couldn't hold back a curious question. Linc rarely spoke about his ex-wife and Chandra wanted to know what the woman had been like and why the marriage hadn't lasted. Perhaps if she did, it would help her to understand Linc better. "What did she enjoy?"

To Chandra's surprise it was Ted who replied, revealing everything with only a few words. "She only liked good things, not good people, and she didn't like kids at all."

No wonder Linc was being so careful. The last thing these little boys needed was someone else rejecting them. When he brought a woman into this home, he needed to be sure she wouldn't ever walk out again.

"Uncle Linc says she didn't let him ride his motorcycle 'cause she was afraid he'd fall off and get hurt, but grandpa says she wanted to put reins on his spirit," Chas piped in. "You'd never do that, would you, Chandra?"

"Do what?" Linc asked as he strode into the room and picked up a dish towel.

Thinking to save Chas from more disciplinary action, Chandra answered for him. "We were talking about how it's wrong to impose your will on other people just because they don't hold the same convictions as you do. I was about to tell Chas that even though I'll worry about your safety during the Hare and Hounds race, I would never tell you I didn't want you to take part. I'll just have to trust that you've got the experience to know what you're doing and will be all right."

Linc didn't look entirely convinced that that was all they had been discussing but he didn't try to verify his suspicions. "I'll be fine, Chandra. I've been riding a motorcycle since I was fourteen," he stated firmly, eyes steady on hers. "Will you be there cheering for me when I cross the finish line?"

"Yes." Her simple declaration brought an astounding reaction.

Making no concessions to the boys, Linc pulled her into his arms and gave her a long and devastatingly thorough kiss. Her knees were like jelly and she was completely out of breath by the time he let her go. The wild flush that pounded in her cheeks was greatly aided by the delighted grins on the faces of the bright-eyed witnesses to their uncle's exuberant assault on her senses.

"Well...we'd better finish up these dishes," she stammered, looking around for the dish towel she had dropped when Linc had dragged her against him.

"We do have to get to bed early tonight, fellas," Linc concurred, taking Ted's place at the sink full of sudsy water. "I want to make an early start tomorrow."

"You're coming too, aren't you, Chandra?" Chas asked as he balanced two glasses in either hand and mimicked a tightrope walker on his way to the opposite counter.

"I haven't issued the invitation yet," Linc broke in before Chandra could ask Chas what he was talking about. "I was hoping to send you guys to bed, then persuade Chandra to come."

"Come where?" Chandra inquired, knowing she wouldn't be able to refuse even if Linc announced he was taking a trip to the dark side of the moon. Chas had already grasped her hand and Ted wore a hopeful expression that made her heart melt, as they both waited for Linc to answer her question.

"We're going camping in the Superior National Forest. You know, battle the elements and live off the land? We'll backpack in tomorrow, spend the night, then hike out again on Sunday. Would you like to come with us?"

Looking at the three sets of eager eyes, Chandra didn't even consider the fact that she hadn't been camping since she was a child and perhaps wouldn't enjoy it nearly as much now. "I'd love to," she asserted enthusiastically.

Hours later, after being the beneficiary of a highly passionate and sensual form of masculine persuasion, she was totally convinced that she wanted nothing more in life than to get up at 6:00 A.M., carry a heavy pack on a long trek through dense forest, then scrounge for sustenance amidst nature's bountiful harvest.

10

"PACK LIGHT," Chandra mumbled disgustedly, remembering Linc's final instructions for their overnight trip. Studying the collection of items she'd heaped in the center of the living-room floor, she knew she'd have to discard most of it. Linc had provided a backpack and she'd been allotted only one of its compartments for her own use. The rest was already packed with sundry camping and fishing gear.

It would be impossible to take all the items she'd tossed together. Linc and the boys would no doubt interpret the accumulation that covered most of the oval braided rug as a typically female approach to camping. "No way!" she announced and began separating her belongings into two piles.

Surely she could sleep one night without a pillow. The down-filled luxury was tossed aside. Pajamas, robe and slippers. *Ridiculous, Chandra! Where is your head?*

Those articles joined the pillow. It was a long time since she'd roughed it in the great outdoors but she'd had plenty of early experience. Her parents had taken her backpacking every summer from the time she was old enough to be one of the items carried in a pack. She knew a thing or two! She eliminated most of the heap and stuffed the remainder into the canvas pack.

Eyeing the discard pile, Chandra decided she'd better get rid of it before Linc arrived. Hurriedly she scooped everything up and headed toward the loft. She didn't want to leave any evidence around—even if she had pointed out the error of her own thinking. This outing was doubtless another one of Linc's tests and she would not fail.

As Chandra clattered upward, laden down with superfluous clothing, a blanket, towels and extra shoes, her cosmetic bag slipped out of the pile and bounced down the stairs. Hearing the clank of the jars within, she resolved to take along at least some of the contents. She could live without the makeup but the skin-care products wouldn't take up much room. Those jars of cleansing cream and moisturizer were essential. Her face would disappear if she used soap.

Soap? Maybe she'd better tuck in a bar of her own. No telling what kind Linc would provide—probably Lava. She hadn't had to worry about such things when she'd earned her camping beads. What did a ten-year-old Camp Fire Girl know about wrinkles and chapping?

The sound of tires crunching on the graveled drive made Chandra's feet move a bit faster up the stairs. She shoved her bundle into the closet and raced back down to retrieve the cosmetic bag. The contents were dumped irreverently on her dresser and the bag repacked, minus all the expensive beauty products. At the last second, she plucked a tube of lipstick from the pile and tossed it in the bag. The creamy concoction would keep her lips from drying out and was therefore a necessity.

Toothbrush! Rumbling back down the stairs in her heavy hiking boots, Chandra grabbed up the brush and a tube of paste from the bathroom. She was just sliding the toiletries between the folds of a sweat shirt when Linc and the boys knocked on the door. She zipped the pack closed, gave it a satisfied pat and answered the summons.

"All ready?" Linc asked as he brushed past her. "This it?" His tone was skeptical, as if to imply that he expected her to bring more than her backpack and sleeping bag. Ted, Chas and Matt, who trailed in after him, wore similarly dubious expressions.

All right, you chauvinists. Suppressing a triumphant grin, Chandra answered innocently, "Of course. It's been a number of years since I've done any camping but I guess it's like riding a bike. You never forget how to pack for a camp-out." She didn't feel at all guilty about failing to mention the stuff she'd just put away. No sense providing the ammunition when it was so blatantly apparent that they had been expecting to shoot her down before the trip had even begun.

Linc studied her carefully for a long minute as if waiting for her to confess that a huge duffel bag of additional gear lurked behind the couch. Feigning a guilty look, she snapped her fingers. "That's right. I did forget something."

She was deeply gratified by the knowing looks that passed between the four males. *Enjoy your little triumph, guys. It won't last long.*

Turning, Chandra crossed to the kitchen area and lifted two small paper bags from the counter. "I know you said we'd live off the land," she offered sheepishly. "But I thought a few apples and cookies might come in handy." She smiled broadly when their smug expressions were replaced by looks of chagrin.

Matt couldn't hold on to the superior male pose any longer. All smiles, he squealed in delight. Turning to his brothers, he announced smugly, "I told you she was okay. The camp-out'll be even better with her along."

"Yes, well...." Linc paused, giving Chandra a tongue-in-cheek glare as he realized she had purposely strung them all. "You could be right, Matt."

Picking up the backpack, Linc handed it to Ted. "Take this on out and load it in the back of the Bronco. Chas, you take her sleeping bag. Matt?" His eyes twinkled as he viewed the look of anticipation on the youngest boy's face. "Think we can trust you to be in charge of the cookies and apples?"

"Sure," Matt said seriously as if he'd just been assigned a task of enormous responsibility. "I'll guard 'em." He trotted out the door behind his brothers, carrying the bags as if they contained royal treasures.

Chandra started to follow Matt out the door. "Not so fast, cookie lady." Linc's low voice stopped her.

When Chandra turned, Linc pulled her against him. "This'll have to last us until Sunday night." He lowered his head and brushed her lips softly before settling his mouth over hers.

Chandra wrapped her arms around his waist and moved farther into his embrace, reveling in the possessive way he held her. One arm held her close while his other hand was buried in her hair, holding her head in place. As always, his kiss was all-consuming, blocking out everything but the taste, feel and scent of him. And, as always, Chandra responded to it, welcoming his tongue into her mouth, then returning the invasion and domination.

"Maybe that wasn't such a good idea," Linc murmured shakily against her ear. "It'll only remind me of what we'd be doing if we spent the weekend alone."

Chandra pressed a kiss into Linc's throat and sighed as she nestled her head against his shoulder. "Pretty sure of yourself, aren't you?"

"Sure am," he answered as he swept her hair aside and nuzzled her neck.

"Are you saying I'm easy?" Chandra asked, pretending indignation but tilting her head aside to expose more of her neck to Linc's wandering mouth.

"Not easy. Just willing." Linc tugged Chandra's blouse loose from the back of her jeans, then slipped his hands beneath and around to her front. He cupped her breasts, his thumbs brushing across their peaks. Chandra's bra, though a practical sports design rather than the delicate lace type she normally wore, provided no real barrier to his touch and her nipples tightened to hard throbbing points.

"As willing as I am," he admitted, then sought her mouth again. Linc's willingness was evident in the hard lines of his body and the hunger of his kiss. They were both breathless and shaking when he released her mouth and rested his forehead against hers.

"Uh . . . there are three boys outside waiting to go camping," Chandra stated weakly.

"They just went camping with Henry a couple of weeks ago." Linc's tone was equally distracted as he dropped kisses on Chandra's eyelids. "Let's call it off and stay here."

"But you promised them," she reminded, though her body was already singing in reaction to Linc's caresses. A few minutes more and she'd be beyond thinking of anything else.

"So I did," he agreed resignedly. "It's going to be a long weekend."

Reluctantly, Chandra pushed out of his arms and tucked her plaid blouse back into her jeans. With more brightness than she was feeling, she urged, "Come on. We'd better get going. It'll take close to an hour to get to Superior National Forest and then we'll have to hike in. We don't want to burn daylight."

Linc nodded but his expression was still petulant. Under his breath he mumbled, "Can't burn it fast enough."

If Chandra hadn't been suffering just as greatly from the ache of denial, she might have laughed. He looked so much like a little boy whose ice cream had just fallen off the cone. Trying to spark his enthusiasm, she remarked, "It's beautiful up there and we're going to have a lot of fun."

"Some fun. I can think of a few more enjoyable things to do than—"

"Hey! This was your idea, remember?" Chandra tossed over her shoulder. Grabbing up her jacket and a wide-brimmed hat, she stepped outside, needing to put as much space between them as possible in order to resist the lingering invitation in his eyes.

"Not one of my better ones," Linc grumbled as he

followed her, checking to make sure the door was locked before he descended the stairs from the deck.

Watching Chandra's retreating backside, he groaned inwardly. She filled out her jeans amazingly well for someone with such a slight figure. The denim was worn and whitened where it skimmed across her softly, rounded behind.

Her sable curls bounced in springy abandon across her shoulders, their rich color in sharp contrast to the citrus-colored plaid of her blouse. The blouse was as bright and sunny as one of her smiles. In the space of two weeks, she'd become the sunshine in his life.

It wasn't as if there had been no bright spots before her arrival. He had the boys and they brought him more joy than any one man deserved. He'd never regretted taking on the responsibility of raising them. As full as he'd thought his life was, it had taken one smart, curly-haired, curvaceous accountant with the softest brown eyes he'd ever seen to point out that something was still missing—a mate.

He loved her, yes, but would that be enough? If he had no one but himself to consider, the decision would be easy. His life wasn't as simple as it had been eight years ago when he'd married Jean.

He checked himself. Chandra wasn't Jean. But there were some similarities. *Take your time*, he cautioned. *You've known the woman only two weeks.* Love might not be enough to sustain a lifelong commitment and he would settle for nothing less. If Chandra couldn't fit into the world he and the boys had built together, it would be better to find out now.

THE HOUR-LONG DRIVE was noisy and boisterous. At times, all three boys were talking at once. Yet amidst all the chatter and even when Chas led them into some hilarious renditions of songs, Chandra sensed a quietness in Linc. Though his resonant baritone joined in the singing and he laughed at the appropriate place, it was as if he was going through the motions while his mind was somewhere else.

She didn't believe he was actually sulking over their not being able to act on their desire. There would be other times, a whole lifetime of them—at least Chandra hoped so. She loved him. He loved her. It was simple. As far as she was concerned, marriage was the obvious answer. All she could do was go on hoping that Linc's logical accountant's mind would eventually lead him to the same conclusion.

"Okay, guys. This is it," Linc announced as he parked the wagon. "We walk the rest of the way."

Everyone was outfitted with a framed pack except Matt, who wore a small schoolbag on his back. They spent a few moments adjusting shoulder and waist straps, then the party of five headed toward a trail leading into the forest. The trail was narrow and they were forced to march along in single file, Linc leading the way and Chandra bringing up the rear.

She tried not to giggle at the comical parade in front of her. The framed packs were so high, she couldn't see anyone's head but Matt's. The others looked like three bundles of khaki canvas with denim legs. The papa pack, the baby packs and the mama pack, she chimed to herself. The mama sounded rather nice. . . .

Only the footworn path gave any indication that

civilization had encroached upon the dense spruce-fir forest. Beyond the narrow trail, the forest floor was carpeted with layer upon layer of needles and clusters of wildflowers grew where the sunlight had penetrated the heavy canopy of green.

The brilliant white blossoms of goldthreads were like patches of diamonds against an emerald setting. The fragrance of shinleafs mingled lightly with the heavier scent of the firs, and with their small waxy rosettes attached to slender, delicate stalks, they resembled domestic lilies of the valley. Here and there pink bell-shaped twinflowers nodded atop their downy stalks, adding accent to the otherwise green, brown and white color scheme of the forest.

Chandra was so taken by the beauty around her that her step slowed to a crawl. When she finally realized how long she had been dawdling, the others were nowhere in sight. Not paying attention, she'd wandered off the unmarked trail. She had no idea how long it had been since she'd left it nor how far she'd gone astray.

She fought the impulse to run. Suddenly, the scene around her lost some of its beauty. The forest seemed to be closing in on her, intent on imprisoning her forever. Chandra had welcomed the cooler temperature and absence of bright sun when she'd first stepped into the forest to investigate a flash of color she'd noticed in the branches of a tree. Now it seemed dank, dark and threatening. She turned around several times. Everything looked the same. She had no idea which way to turn. Every minute seemed like a year and she feared she was walking in circles.

As time passed, Chandra felt a tight knot of sheer

panic settle in her stomach. What if she became injured somehow and no one could find her for days? What if she were threatened by wolves or attacked by bears? She was ready to scream in helpless terror before she remembered her childhood lessons.

Listen with all your senses, not just with your ears, and the forest will tell you all you need to know. She brushed away a tear and went still, opening herself totally to the stimuli around her.

Blending with the soughing of the firs as they swayed in the wind far above the forest floor was the tapping of a woodpecker. The drawling, buzzy song of a boreal chicadee called from above her left shoulder. The raucous voice of a blue jay could be heard over the softer sounds, a dissonant cry amidst the harmony.

Chandra smiled in relief and moved in the direction of the jay's scolding cry. Undisturbed on a high perch and hidden by foliage, jays sang a whisper song of faint whistles and soft, sweet notes. But when their territory was invaded in any way, they set up a ruckus that shattered the peaceful composition of pastoral music floating through the forest. Chandra kept her fingers crossed that the bird's territory had been invaded by four humans rather than just another jay.

A few minutes later she was back on the trail. She tuned all her senses on the irritated squawking, growing more and more certain it was a protest against the presence of one large man and three small boys. Sure enough, when she came around a huge boulder, she spied Linc and the boys resting beneath a tall tamarack.

"You could've called out," Chandra reproved huffily, feeling like joining forces with the furious jay.

"We didn't know you were missing until a few minutes ago when we stopped to rest," Linc offered as an excuse, but Chandra clearly felt he was guilty of negligence. "I would have called out but your champion here—" he thumbed toward Matt "—said that you'd find us. Matt claims that Henry taught you how to listen to the wind. Is that right or did you just get lucky?"

Chandra wanted to wipe the grin off Linc's face but she was too relieved to have found them to hold on to her irritation. "A little of both, I think." She nodded toward the treetops. "Your friend up there was a big help."

As she drew closer, she saw that Linc's grin didn't quite reach his eyes. He had been worried. The blue depths registered relief not humor. Seeing the soft look on his face, she fought tears. Now that she was safe, she wanted to be held and pour out her fears within the sanctuary of his arms. Linc seemed to know that for, wordlessly, he opened them to her.

"It's silly to cry now," she muttered into his shirt-front. "I didn't cry when I was lost. I didn't mean to get lost. It was all so beautiful. I forgot to watch the trail. What'll the boys think?"

"They'll think you're very human," Linc assured gently, folding his arms around her. "The important thing is that you're safe and you remembered not to panic when you couldn't find us." He rubbed his palms up and down her arms, soothing her as much with his touch as with his words.

"Hey. It's okay, Chandra," a young voice confirmed from beside her.

Chandra lifted her face from Linc's chest, surprised to see that it was Ted who was offering sympathy. "Thanks, Ted," Chandra acknowledged. "Probably what you'd expect from a woman, right?" she asked, trying to inject a little humor in her tone while offering a tremulous smile.

"Naw. I got lost once and I just sat down and started bawling my head off until grandpa found me." Ted kept his attention on his toe, drawing circles in the spruce needles as he described the incident.

"Oh, Ted, you don't know how close I came to doing just that." She gave his shoulder a soft squeeze. "Thanks." She knew it hadn't been easy for him to divulge the information and appreciated what the admission had cost him. "If I hadn't found you guys by now, I would've set up a howl."

"Speaking of howling," Linc broke in. "We'd better get going or we'll all be howling for lunch before we've set up camp."

They started off again. This time Ted volunteered to bring up the rear and Chandra didn't argue with him. They reached a clearing not too much farther up the trail that Linc deemed the perfect campsite. Duties were quickly assigned and everyone went to work. Within an hour, Linc was doling out sandwiches.

At first sight of the peanut-butter-and-jellied bread, packed in plastic bags and served with crisp celery and carrot sticks, Chandra raised her brows in quiet amusement. "No cracks," Linc warned. "We'll live off the land for the next meal."

And so they did, or rather they relied on a nearby stream. The clear water that tumbled and frothed over and around its rock-strewed bed yielded a string of trout. The rest of the meal was straight off the shelves of a camping-supply store—dehydrated foods sealed in long-life packets. Once the contents were dropped in boiling water, a delicately flavored rice pilaf, green beans and mixed fruit appeared. Chandra managed to turn the fruit into a respectable cobbler with the addition of a thick crust made from biscuit mix.

"That was delicious," Linc pronounced, licking the last of his cobbler off a spoon. "This camp-out promises to be a lot better with you along." The slow sexy grin he directed toward Chandra indicated he was commenting on far more than her cooking prowess. "A lot better," he reiterated, his voice a low, rough drawl.

Now that was a heated gaze if ever there was one, Chandra thought as she quickly turned her face back toward the campfire. The heat in her cheeks and rushing through her entire torso had nothing to do with the flames flickering along the burning logs.

When they began setting up camp and only two tents appeared, Chandra had thrown Linc a puzzled look. He'd shrugged before explaining, "They're two-man tents and the boys are small enough to fit into one without any trouble."

Remembering the excuse he'd used to sweep her into his arms and kiss her nearly senseless before the trip even began, Chandra had blurted, "But you—"

"I wasn't thinking straight, so early in the morning," he'd supplied, obviously having guessed her thoughts. "Have to be practical when you backpack. No sense lugging along three tents when two's enough. You don't mind sharing one with me, do you?" he'd asked, a picture of innocence before his grin had turned into a leer and his eyebrows had waggled comically.

Chandra knew if she sneaked a peek over her shoulder again, she'd probably see that same leer. He'd kept her continually on edge all afternoon. The looks he'd given her were enough to melt her bones but that wasn't all he'd had in his armory. This man she'd once foolishly labeled shy, perhaps afraid of women, was well outfitted with a full magazine of double entendres that had taxed her wits to counter without sounding like a blithering idiot.

Not content with words and the sensual communication of his eyes, he'd trailed his fingers down her spine, squeezed her bottom whenever the boys couldn't see what he was doing and topped it all off by blowing in her ear while both of her hands were occupied pulling in a struggling trout. He'd been darn lucky that she hadn't thrown his expensive rod and reel into the stream and taken him up on his invitation right there in front of the boys.

What was the man thinking of? Feeling a sudden rush of warmth, Chandra pictured what he was thinking. She couldn't understand why he was being such a tease.

She had come on this camping trip thinking it was a chance for her to prove that she really did enjoy roughing it, and wanted to spend time with the boys, but now she wasn't so sure. It seemed more like a challenge of her stamina and her ability to withstand the physical attraction between her and Linc.

Chandra swatted at a mosquito, thankful for the distraction. "Better get these dishes done," she said and reached for the steaming kettle.

"Let's set up the washing brigade, boys," Linc instructed. "We all wash our own mess kits out here. Right, guys?"

With a minimum of grumbling, Ted and Chas gathered up their utensils. However, Matt was almost asleep, propped against a tree trunk. He rubbed at his eyes with his chubby hands and yawned widely.

The little boy offered only a token protest when Chandra started removing the sticky remains of supper from his face and hands with a soapy cloth. When she was finished, he was leaning against her for support. Automatically, she scooped him up and started carrying him across the clearing to the boys' tent.

As they passed the dishwashing station, Linc lightly captured her around the shoulders. "Good night, tiger," he said and leaned around Chandra to place a brief kiss on Matt's forehead. "Say good-night to your brothers."

"Night." Matt's farewell was muffled against Chandra's shoulder and his brothers' answering calls didn't indicate a great deal more energy.

Crawling into the tent with Matt, Chandra removed his shoes and helped him into his sleeping bag. Kneeling next to him, she brushed a lock of hair from his forehead and leaned over to kiss him. Immediately, his chubby little arm came around her neck. "Night, Aunt Chandra," he offered in a soft whisper.

Chandra blinked away a tear and buried her face in his silky hair. "Good night, sweetheart," she whispered as she cuddled him for another minute before gently lowering his shoulders and tucking his sleeping bag around him. She stayed a little longer to assure herself he was asleep as well as to get a grip on her emotions. *Aunt Chandra.* It had a nice sound.

Back outside, she discovered that the kitchen crew had finished up. Linc handed her a cup of coffee. "Some of nature's bounty or another surprise from your magic knapsack?" she teased as she wrapped her hands around the enameled mug.

"You'd rather I boiled some roots or leaves for a tea?"

Stepping back and guarding her coffee, Chandra quickly demurred. "No, no. I wasn't complaining. I far prefer the coffee." Taking a sip, she was delighted to discover it was generously laced with sugar. "Mmm, just the way I like it," she purred, savoring the sweet hot drink as well as the knowledge that Linc had remembered how she liked her coffee.

The forest around them was giving up the day and settling into the night. Beyond the circle of flickering light cast by the fire and the small lantern Linc had hung from a tree branch, all was black. Instead of being frightening, it seemed comforting, as if a protective wall had been thrown up around their little campsite. Linc pulled out a harmonica and provided the accompaniment for singing. At first the songs were lively, but it wasn't long before the tempo slowed and Ted and Chas were doing more yawning than singing.

Once the boys were settled in for the night, Linc

turned the lantern down low, then made himself comfortable on the ground beside Chandra. He draped his arm around her and she nestled her head against his shoulder. They sat contentedly together, sipping their coffee, staring at the fire and listening to the peaceful night sounds.

"You're actually enjoying all this, aren't you?" Linc asked, his voice hushed and his tone easy.

"You sound a bit surprised," Chandra responded quietly, too relaxed and content to feel any irritation at the query.

His gaze directed at the fire, Linc took a sip of his coffee before divulging, "Let's say I had a few doubts. Hiking around in the woods and keeping track of three boys isn't the kind of outing a lot of women would enjoy."

"I'm not a lot of women. In case you haven't noticed, I'm just one—me."

"Oh, I'm very aware of that," Linc drawled and snuggled her closer. He set his empty mug down on the log that was supporting their backs and gently turned her toward him. "You seem pretty comfortable casting a fly rod and cooking over an open fire."

Without warning, he took her hat from her head and tossed it aside, then buried his hands in the rich, silky thickness of her hair. Urging her face closer to his, he held her gaze. "How experienced are you at necking around a campfire?"

"You'll just have to find out for yourself," she challenged in a whisper just before Linc's lips covered hers.

His kiss was gentle, with none of the urgency and demand of the morning. Instead he seemed content to tantalize, running the tip of his tongue along the outline of her lips for what seemed like an eternity. His tender, nonstop caresses lulled her into limp acquiescence, and his touch was light as he gathered her slowly closer. Not until he finally raised his head did Chandra discover he'd neatly unzipped her sweat shirt and unbuttoned her blouse.

Like a whisper, his lips moved down her throat while his fingertips teased across the tops of her breasts, then insinuated themselves beneath her bra. "You've definitely had some experience at this," Chandra murmured breathlessly as he teased her nipples.

"Maybe," Linc said casually, but his breathing indicated that he was not as unmoved as he might like her to think.

Two could play at that game, Chandra decided, and while Linc's attention was focused on the tender torture of her throat and breasts, she unfastened the buttons of his shirt and pushed up the T-shirt beneath. Her fingertips began their own delicate grazing across his chest, paying special attention to the whorls of curling hair around his nipples. He'd teased and seduced her all day and Chandra was determined to get some of her own back, forgetting that it was a two-way street. As she aroused him, he returned the favor and each other's quickened response was in itself stimulating.

When she drew a line with one fingernail down his chest, around his navel and along the waistband of his jeans, Linc returned his mouth to hers. No gentle persuasion this time but a thorough possession.

As their kiss deepened and intensified, their hands

moved more boldly. Linc ran his hand along the curve of her hip and then between her thighs, rocking his palm against the juncture until Chandra was quivering with need. Not content to be idle, she rubbed her palm along the front of his jeans, curving over the hard virile outline that throbbed beneath.

"This isn't enough. I'm going to explode," Linc rasped and in one fluid motion was on his feet. Scooping Chandra up into his arms, he strode to their tent.

Feverishly, their trembling fingers tore at boot-laces, zippers and buttons. Finally freed of all barriers, they fell naked together onto their opened sleeping bags. Without preamble, Linc sheathed himself deep in Chandra's waiting warmth, immediately setting a rapid rhythm that she met. Wrapping her legs around his surging hips, she clung to him as she rode a crest of ecstasy.

With a shudder and a cry muffled against her shoulder, Linc erupted within her. They lay entwined tightly, holding each other until they became conscious of the chill night air. Not breaking their unity completely, Linc rose to his knees, flipped back the top sleeping bag and slipped them both beneath the downy covers.

Pressing his lips against her temple, he said, "I'm sorry that was so fast. I haven't been that impatient for years. I promise I'll make it up to you as soon as I recover." His hands were already making a foray over her body and his maleness pushed boldly and hotly between her thighs.

"You weren't the only one who was impatient," Chandra whispered, feeling a rush of renewed excitement mingle with the aftertremors of their climax. "You've been seducing me since six o'clock this morning."

"I'm ascared."

The high-pitched cry accompanied the opening of the tent flap. Matt came tumbling in, landing on Linc's back, which flattened him down upon Chandra. Linc and Chandra stared wide-eyed at each other. Desire evaporated.

Carefully, Linc rolled aside and sat up. "Wh-what scared you?" he managed to get out.

"Don't know," Matt said as he wrapped his arms in a death grip around Linc's neck. "Maybe a bear or . . . or a mountain lion," he supplied in awestruck tones. "Can I stay here with you and Aunt Chandra?"

Chandra fumbled around in the scattered clothing until she found her blouse. She slipped it on and discreetly searched for her panties and jeans. She wasn't sure whether she should be embarrassed or start laughing. There was very little light sifting through the tent's walls from the lantern outside, but it was enough for her to see Linc's expression. Over Matt's shoulder, he sent her a look of pure frustration.

"Uncle Linc. You don't have any clothes on. Were you hot or something?"

"That about covers it," Linc muttered, sending Chandra off into a fit of giggles.

CHANDRA RODE IN THE TRUCK WITH LINC on the way to the Hare and Hounds race while Henry and the boys followed behind them in the Bronco wagon. It was only a ten-mile drive and there wasn't much time to talk. Even if there had been, Linc wasn't in the mood for a heavy discussion, and Chandra realized that it wasn't the time to bring up the subject of her upcoming departure.

In the week following the camping trip, she had completed the audit at Hammond. She had learned from Karen that she was needed in Chicago to deal with one of their small, longtime clients who refused to work with anyone else. She'd made arrangements to fly back to the city on Monday morning. Linc was well aware of her plans but as yet had said nothing to make her think he was going to propose before she left town. She hoped he was only waiting until the race was over to correct that omission.

She knew how long Linc had been practicing for the worthwhile charity event and felt sure that once it was behind him, he would focus all his attention on plans for their future together. She had passed every one of his ridiculous tests with flying colors and now all that was left for them to do was work out the logistics. Since falling in love with him, Chandra had devoted a lot of time to the task of coming up with a viable means of combining her work with the responsibilities of marriage and raising a family.

It would take a few weeks back in Chicago to arrange everything, but she was almost positive that Karen would support the conclusions she'd reached. For years the woman had been saying that Chandra should find herself a good man and get married. Chandra hoped she'd still feel that way even if it would mean the end of their partnership.

She knew Linc wouldn't expect her to give up her career and she wouldn't have to if he agreed to what she had in mind. A good C.P.A. could always find clients and operate anywhere. She could set up an office and function out of her new home. That way she would have the dual pleasure of doing the work she loved and being there for the boys whenever they needed her. At tax time, things might get a bit hectic, but with two accountants in the family she was sure it wouldn't be a problem.

Chandra could hardly wait for the race to be over so she and Linc could work out the details together. She gave a small sigh as she looked over at him and noted that his mind was occupied with thoughts that had absolutely nothing to do with her. His hands squeezed and released the steering wheel as if practicing for the time when they'd be adjusting around the leather grips on his bike. He didn't appear to be nervous exactly but rather having difficulty suppressing an explosive inner energy.

"I'm still not sure I fully understand how this kind of race works," Chandra said, smothering a giggle as Linc jumped. Evidently he had completely forgotten she was there. Resigned to the fact that there would be no personal discussions until much later in the day, she asked, "Won't there be any course laid out?"

"Actually a Hare and Hounds race is just a polite way of referring to a free-for-all. But, even with all the mayhem, it's great," Linc declared enthusiastically as he turned the truck off the highway onto an unmarked, graveled road. "There will be about thirty of us trying to get across the finish line first. When the race is over the sponsors and those who've made it to the end will go out looking for the riders who suffered mechanical failure or couldn't negotiate the terrain and stalled out. Dragging all those machines out of the woods will take a couple of hours. Sometimes that's more fun than the race itself."

"You call that fun?" Chandra inquired, shaking her head in disbelief. She would never understand this kind of fun but could see that Linc truly believed what he'd said.

"It's the same principle as camping or mountain climbing," Linc observed smoothly as he pointed ahead to the line of trucks, cars and motorcycles parading up the road. "All these guys have come out today to match wits with Mother Nature in a way. Successfully negotiating all the twists and turns that wily old lady has to offer on her turf gives you the greatest high in the world. Some of us will make it, some of us won't and those who don't will come up with the most outlandish excuses you've ever heard."

"Like what?"

"I heard one guy say after an enduro race that he would have won it but he ran into a cow who was in labor and stopped to give the poor animal a helping hand. But the best excuse I ever heard was from one of the pros. He said he was so sure he was going to win that he visualized going over the finish line before he really got there. Couldn't figure out why no one would give him the winner's cup."

Linc's eyes twinkled with laughter as he read Chandra's incredulous expression. "You should have seen Joe after winning a race. He wouldn't come down for days. Rebecca told me they once had to move their trailer in the middle of the night because Joe woke up all the neighbors with his victory dance. I wish he was here for this. That would've made it a real contest. Compared to him, these guys don't even know how to ride."

"Hey, you're not out to prove something, are you?" Chandra couldn't help asking the question that had been niggling at her ever since Ted had made the statement that Linc was a good driver but couldn't compare with his father. "To the boys?"

"Like what?" Linc looked genuinely confused.

Chandra chose her words carefully, not wanting to anger him before the race. He would need total concentration to make it through the course and she didn't want to say anything that might upset him. "I know Joe was a professional biker and a very good one. Ted showed me all the awards he won when he was racing. I know you love riding and I hope you've entered this race for that reason, not because you feel you have to prove to the boys that you're just as good as their father was."

Linc's loud bark of laughter put an instant end to her fears. "If I needed to prove that, I would have stayed on the racing circuit when I was young enough to enjoy abusing my body. I envied Joe his natural ability but we were never rivals. He had an extra something that drove him to take risks I never wanted to take. I expect the boys to admire their father for what he was and me for what I am."

"They love you, Linc," Chandra said softly. "Whether you race or not wouldn't alter that."

"I'm racing today because I want to help get the Culture Exchange off the ground. Joe would've wanted the boys to learn all they could about their heritage. I vowed I'd do that for him and that's why competing in this race is so important to me. The Chippewa have been in danger of forgetting their history. That's not going to happen if I have anything to say about it."

He gave her an insulted glance. "I may not be a pro but I'm not a half-bad driver. You may not know this but I won the Duluth Invitational Motocross two years in a row."

"How old were you?"

"Eighteen, but I've still got a few good jumps left in me," Linc insisted in a disgruntled tone.

"Geronimo, hotshot!" Chandra slid across the seat and gave Linc a loud smack on the cheek. "I love you, Gold Spear. If I may quote from that wise old Indian, Little Bear, hell, we're gonna win this baby standing still."

An hour later, Chandra had hoisted Matt atop her shoulders so he could see the motorcycles race away once the starting gun went off. What happened after that was a scene she would never forget. Looking like a multicolored swarm of angry bees, the racers zoomed across an open field, down a dirt incline, then up the other side and around a muddy track that led into the forest. At least six of the bikes never made it to the woods.

Three riders slid off their seats on the way up the steep grade and two more got stuck in the mud. Another rider tried to take a shortcut around a dense thicket of shrubbery and ended up entangled in the barbed branches. Chandra's concern for Linc's safety was greatly eased when she saw that none of the riders eliminated from the race was hurt. From where she was standing on the far side of the field she could hear plenty of colorful language but no one was calling for first-aid.

Linc was wearing a bright yellow jump suit and his black helmet so he was easy to spot amidst the throng of bikers that zigzagged through the trees. He shared the lead with four other racers, but Chandra had complete confidence that when the race was over he would be the only one occupying that position. She could already tell that the practice sessions he had put in on her property were paying off. He rode like the wind, negotiating the sharp turns with ease and flying over the man-made water hazards with the expertise of a soaring eagle.

"Coming with us to the next checkpoint, Chandra?" Henry called as he opened the door of the wagon. "They'll be out of sight in another couple of minutes. It'll be a bumpy ride but we might catch up with them when they cross Tallmidge Creek."

Since Matt was far more interested in a nearby snow-cone vendor than the race, Chandra elected to stay behind and await the outcome in relative comfort. Linc had arranged some folding chairs in the back of the truck and brought a cooler with sandwiches and soft drinks. Matt was perfectly content to sit on the tailgate and nibble at his cherry cone while Chandra absorbed the festive atmosphere around her.

The field had been fenced off by strings of gaily-colored flags, and now that the racers had entered the woods the spectators milled about in the open space, trying to catch a glimpse of them through the trees. The whole area resembled a campground, but people had set up temporary residences in a variety of vans and trucks instead of tents. Hawkers strolled through the throng, selling beer, hot dogs, candy and soda pop.

"Hi, Matt," a slender, black-haired woman said as she hopped up in the truck and held out her hand to Chandra. "Linc wanted me to come over and introduce myself. I'm Racine Whitewater. My husband Ned is one of the other contestants."

"Nice to meet you." Chandra smiled as they shook hands. "I'm Chandra Collins. Are you the Racine Whitewater who owns that marvelous restaurant off Highway 9?"

"One and the same," the woman declared, her smile growing wider at the compliment. "Not everyone would agree that it's marvelous but we do have some pretty loyal supporters. Linc for one. He not only eats there himself as often as he can but he keeps bringing over new people to try it out."

"That's how I discovered it," Chandra replied. "I wasn't too sure I was going to like it but Linc persuaded me to give it a try and now I'd recommend it to anyone. The food is delicious."

"Thanks. Linc's done a lot for us," Racine said, her

brown eyes soft with affection. "If he hadn't cosigned our business loan, we never would have opened."

Somehow Racine's disclosure about the loan didn't surprise Chandra. She'd already realized that Linc was very loyal to his friends and would do anything for them. The two women were of similar age and were soon talking like old friends.

It was almost twenty minutes later when Racine said that she had to rejoin her two young daughters, who were jumping up and down in the back of a truck parked a few yards away. Several times as the race progressed the names of the leaders would be announced over a loudspeaker, and a resounding cheer would rise up in the crowd.

Chandra and Racine exchanged excited waves each time Linc's or Ned's number was called but their voices couldn't be heard over the din. When Henry, Chas and Ted returned to report that Linc and Ned were neck and neck going through the last checkpoint, the Rainclouds and the Whitewaters became the two loudest cheering sections in the place.

In the end, however, just as Chandra had expected, it was Linc who came charging around the last curve far ahead of everyone else. He held up both arms as he broke the ribbon across the finish line, then took a victory lap around the field as the crowd roared its approval. The next few minutes were a chaotic blur.

Swept along through the crowd by Chas and Ted, Chandra was somehow standing all alone when Linc completed his lap and rolled to a stop in the winner's circle. In seconds, he had dismounted and thrown off his helmet. Chandra was lifted off her feet and whirled round and round. Then Linc planted a kiss on her lips that lasted so long the crowd began another round of loud cheering in appreciation of his astounding endurance.

"I hoped you'd be standing here waiting for me," Linc murmured feelingly when he finally allowed her feet to touch the ground. Stepping back, and grinning at her through the grimy streaks of sweat that trailed down his face, he pronounced, "That kiss was better than any trophy they could give me."

"I'm so proud of you," Chandra proclaimed honestly. Then, unmindful that they were making a spectacle of themselves, she threw her arms around his neck. "You deserve one more for good measure."

The second kiss gained them an even louder ovation than the first and it didn't end until they heard Chas's disgruntled mutter, "Aah mush. No girl's gonna kiss me like that when I start winnin' races."

Chandra laughed, then moved aside as Linc was tackled by his three most avid fans. The boys were ecstatic, and even Henry offered the deserving winner a bone-cracking bear hug. An hour later time was called, and the race was declared officially over. All the finishers then got back on their bikes to go and search out those fallen comrades who hadn't made it back to the field. As Linc had predicted, that process took up most of the remainder of the afternoon. After a brief awards ceremony and a speech by a representative of the Indian Action Committee declaring the event a huge success, the crowd drifted away to their cars and trucks.

All in all, it had been a fun but extremely long and tiring day. Again the boys went with Henry, and

Chandra rode in the truck with Linc but on the return trip the front seat was also occupied by a two-foot-tall, gold-plated trophy. Since no one wanted to cook supper, they stopped in at a roadside drive-in restaurant and had hamburgers.

By the time they reached home, all three boys were half asleep. Chandra got them tucked into bed while Linc took a shower and changed clothes. Before turning out the light in the boys' bedroom, she lingered at the door for several moments. A huge lump gathered in her throat as she surveyed the dark heads of the three sleeping children.

If everything worked out, in a very short while she could really start treating them as if they were her own. She already loved them and couldn't wait for the day when they would tell her that they loved her too. She hugged that thought to her breast as she descended the stairs and went to wait for Linc in the living room.

She smiled as she saw the pot of coffee and tray of cookies Henry had set out for them before going home. He'd left shortly after dispatching the boys upstairs. Chandra strongly suspected that Henry knew she was hoping Linc would ask her to marry him tonight and was making sure they'd have ample time alone.

Knowing he was in favor of the match made Chandra feel very good. If Henry thought she could fit in well with the family, then there was every reason to believe that Linc did too. When she left tomorrow, it would be with the knowledge that she would be warmly welcomed when she came back. Even so, the days she would spend away from Linc and the boys wouldn't pass fast enough.

Chandra had almost decided to go home and change into something more attractive than her sleeveless pink blouse and jeans when Linc joined her. She felt considerably better about her casual outfit when she saw that he'd put on a clean pair of jeans and a plaid, short-sleeved shirt. "Hail the conquering hero," she said, nodding her head deferentially as she offered him a chocolate-chip cookie.

"This conquering hero has aches and pains on his aches and pains," Linc complained. He took her hand instead of the cookie, then gingerly lowered himself down beside her on the leather couch. "It's tough getting old. Total bed rest is looking good to me right now. How about you?"

"Sorry." Chandra wrinkled her nose at him. "But I happen to be in my prime. I could be persuaded to give an old man like you some tender loving care but not before we get a few other matters squared away. You are aware that I've got a ten-o'clock flight tomorrow morning?"

Linc ogled her suggestively as he wolfed down the cookie. "After a lengthy massage, I might even be limber enough to drive you to the airport."

This conversation isn't going in the direction I had in mind, Chandra thought, but had a hard time resisting the sensual power in Linc's glittering blue eyes. She forced herself to be strong. If they were ever going to do any serious talking, it had to be tonight. After that it would be at least three weeks before she'd see him again.

Chandra took a deep breath and came out with what had been on her mind all week. "Before I get on that plane tomorrow, Linc, I'd like to know where I stand."

Linc cocked his head and lifted one brow. "I love you. You know that."

Chandra spoke quietly. "Yes, I know, but does that mean you'll...?" She hesitated. If she said much more she'd be the one proposing to him. She thought a moment longer, then decided nothing ventured, nothing gained. It wasn't a leap year but she was a modern woman who could break with tradition and go after what she wanted.

Her features became very solemn as she held his gaze. "Will you marry me, Linc? When I get back from Chicago, will you become my husband?"

His reaction was barely any reaction at all. He blinked, swallowed hard, then looked down at the rug. He didn't say anything for so long that Chandra thought she was going to scream. When he finally did speak, she almost cried out in pain.

"No, Chandra. I won't."

"I see," Chandra choked out, her throat closing up so tightly she couldn't seem to get out any more words. She looked away to hide the swift rush of tears to her eyes, and stared sightlessly at the stone fireplace across the room.

"Three weeks isn't nearly enough time to decide about making a lifelong commitment," Linc expanded on his negative response. "I wouldn't be living up to my responsibilities as a parent if I married you before being absolutely certain it would work."

"And right now you aren't certain it would?" Chandra managed, calling upon all of her willpower to get through what she now knew was going to be the hardest conversation she had ever undertaken in her life.

"No, I'm not. And how can you be?" Linc asked, his tone a plea for understanding. Reaching out for one of her hands, he began stroking the soft skin of her palm. "You've never been married, Chandra, but I know that something you think is really good can just fall apart. I married Jean before I knew enough about her and spent the next five years regretting it. I won't do that again, not to myself or to you."

"So what do you propose we do?" Chandra forced herself to look him in the eye.

"We keep seeing each other until we know for sure our being together is what we both want."

"How are we going to do that?" Chandra pulled her hand out of his grasp to stop the sensual tremors he was creating with his touch. "The only reason I was planning to come back here in three weeks was because I thought I'd be attending a wedding—our wedding. I can't flit back and forth from Chicago just to date you, Linc. I've got a responsibility to my office and my clients, to my partner Karen."

With a cruelty she would never have believed him capable of, he bit out, "If you can't fit me into your busy schedule now, how do you think you'd manage it if we were married? I won't have another woman in my life who puts her job ahead of everything else. The boys went through that once. I won't put them through it again."

"That's unfair!" Chandra jumped up from the couch. "I've shown you in every way I know how that I love you and the boys. I've passed all of the stupid tests you devised to see if I'd make a good wife and a fit mother. What more do you want from me?"

Linc stood up too but made no attempt to touch

her. "I want you to wait until we're both sure that what we've got is good enough to last."

"And you're not sure now?" Chandra's tone was flat, without any emotion.

"Not yet, no." Linc dragged one hand through his hair. "We've got to use some sense. Chandra, I can't—"

"Don't say any more, Linc." Chandra turned away from him and began walking toward the front door. With her hand safely on the handle, she looked back, the depths of her bitterness and hurt shadowing her dark eyes. "I thought I had finally found the person I wanted to share my life with, but it looks as if I was wrong. The man I want will have to love me with his heart, not his head. That might not make any sense to you, Linc, but it makes perfect sense to me."

He took a step toward her but she held up one hand. "No. I don't want you to touch me. When you do, I forget that your kind of love only lasts until you get out of my bed. I never put you through any tests, Linc. I loved you for yourself and didn't expect you to be anyone else."

"Chandra, I'm not trying to make you into someone else," Linc vowed, unable to accept that she was really about to walk out on him. "Come back here so we can discuss this rationally."

Chandra opened the door. "My feelings for you aren't rational so there's nothing to talk about. I can't put love on a balance sheet and measure the pros and cons, nor can I put it on hold until all the kinks are worked out. I loved you enough to trust that they would."

On a last, agonized breath, she accused, "I wish you could trust too, but since you can't I guess you're very right about us. What we've got just isn't good enough to last."

12

LINC LOOSENED HIS TIE and unbuttoned his shirt as he wandered through the empty house. Where was everybody? Henry's truck was parked outside so Linc could only conclude that he and the boys had gone for a walk and would no doubt be back soon.

Linc was tired, hungry and in a foul mood. Finding everybody gone didn't help matters any. He'd come home hoping to catch a quick bite, square arrangements with Henry and the boys, then hightail it to Chicago.

Probably being a damned fool but I've got to do something, Linc grumbled to himself as he entered the kitchen, pulled a bottle of Scotch from the cupboard and sloshed a healthy jigger into a glass.

He drank it neat, hoping the fiery liquid would take the edge off the coldness he'd felt for the past three weeks. A chilling gloom had surrounded him since Chandra had left town. It was as if she'd taken all the sunshine with her. Even the boys felt it, for they dragged listlessly around the house whenever they weren't snapping and snarling at one another. Worse than that were the glares they cast in Linc's direction.

Henry hadn't been any help either. He'd never missed a chance to drop a none-too-subtle hint about

the lonely winters of a man's life, not taking the right
path at the crossroads and other similar comments.
When he'd gone so far as to point out that *shogonos*
weren't smart enough to hang onto a good woman,
Linc had exploded and told him to mind his own
business. Instead of taking offense, the older man
had merely smiled.

That incident had occurred the evening before and
Linc had stormed out of the house. Working out his
anger, he'd taken a long walk—a walk that led him to
Chandra's deserted cabin. He'd spent the greater part
of the night sitting on her deck, thinking about her.

During those long hours, he'd come to the realization that three weeks away from her had done nothing to dampen his desire for her, the need to hear her
voice, enjoy her rich laughter. There were no guaran-
tees about a future with Chandra but he was fast
coming to the realization that it would be miserable
without her. His body as well as his heart ached
every time he thought about her. Hell, every time
he'd seen a woman with dark, curly hair, he'd broken
out into a sweat.

Having finally decided the only way to salvage
what was left of his sanity was to go after Chandra,
Linc had stumbled home and grabbed a few hours'
sleep before going to work. He'd gone through the
day counting the hours until he'd be free to take some
action. Since his mind refused to concentrate on anything but Chandra, he'd given up getting any work
accomplished and left his office two hours early.

Chandra might very likely tell him to take a leap
into Lake Michigan when he presented his proposal
but he was determined to wear her resistance down

no matter how long it took. Even acting the fool was better than sitting around brooding like a hero in a Brontë novel. He loved her. It was pure and simple. He now knew they belonged together and somehow he'd find a way to convince her of that.

He started to pour himself another drink, then decided against it. He had a long drive to the airport ahead of him and needed a clear head. Looking across the room, he noticed the kitchen table was covered with an unfamiliar tablecloth and was already set for six. He groaned. They must be having a guest for dinner and he'd forgotten all about it. By the look of things, it was somebody special for there was a vase of flowers in the middle of the table.

He'd been so numb with exhaustion, he hadn't even noticed the mouth-watering scent filling the room. Checking the oven, he saw a brace of stuffed chickens resting in a roasting pan. Henry was really outdoing himself, Linc mused, as he closed the oven door. He couldn't ever remember his exhibiting such culinary skill. It looked more like something Linc's mother would prepare.

Mom! That was it. His parents had mentioned something about paying them a visit. Even though they had sold the farm and bought a house in Minneapolis, they came back often. They must have driven up for the weekend. That would explain the tablecloth and flowers and why no one was around. Dad had written that he'd bought a new car and he was probably showing it off by giving everybody a ride.

His parents couldn't have picked a worse time to drop in; Linc didn't intend to spend the rest of the day socializing. All he wanted to do was take a short nap, grab a quick bite to eat, then take off. He surely didn't want to waste time trying to explain everything to his parents. He'd tell them later—when he could introduce them to a new daughter-in-law. Admitting to Henry and the boys that he'd been a fool and was about to make a repeat performance this weekend was enough. He didn't feel like informing his parents that they had a lovesick masochist for a son.

He took the two flights of stairs to the third level and strode briskly down the hall toward the master bedroom. It would be better to leave a note saying he was going to Chicago and be on his way before they all got back. It was the coward's way out, but it would certainly save him from confronting some embarrassing questions.

One foot inside his room, Linc stopped dead in his tracks. A stack of cardboard cartons was banked against one wall. A computer table heaped with several more cartons and flanked by a four-drawer filing cabinet took up what had once been an empty corner. "What the . . .?" He raked his fingers through his hair as he slowly turned and took inventory.

Completely dumbfounded he crossed to his bed, stumbling over a pair of slippers—women's slippers! He lowered himself to the king-size mattress and clutched at the spread, coming up with a handful of soft pink nylon rather than the rough cotton weave he'd expected. Unconsciously, he lifted the feminine garment and buried his face in it. Chandra! He breathed in her scent, his mind forming instant images of her wearing nothing but this short wrap that morning by the lake.

He blinked several times, sure that at any moment all this would evaporate like a mirage, but it didn't. He hadn't lost his mind. She'd moved in!

The woman's things were everywhere! A piece of luggage holding clothes he recognized as hers lay open near his dresser. A flowered cosmetic bag sat on the lavatory counter in the adjoining bathroom. The ceramic tiles around the tub were still wet from someone's recent shower and the fragrance of Chandra's perfume mingled with soap to fill the moist air with a sensual scent so powerful that Linc trembled.

CHANDRA WHEELED HER CAR into the driveway and parked it beside Linc's Bronco. This wasn't working out quite as she'd planned it. How dare he come home from work so early? She'd expected to have plenty of time to change, fix her hair and apply a little makeup after she, Henry and the boys returned the U-Haul trailer. That she'd taken the time to shower was some consolation. At least she wouldn't be sweaty when she met him.

"Courage," Henry stated and completely surprised her by squeezing her hand. "Your heart can be trusted. It led you back here. You and Linc have been at the crossroads long enough, and now it is time to walk the same path."

"I don't know, Henry," Chandra hedged. "Maybe I should have called first, talked to him. He didn't want me three weeks ago and nothing has really changed."

"Too late now," Henry told her and pointed to the door. The boys were already out of the car, up the steps and entering the house. "Those blabbermouths are going to tell him for you."

"Maybe I should just wait here and see what happens." She vacillated, fingering her car keys.

It had made so much sense back in Chicago, where she'd gone through a miserable two weeks before deciding to take control of her life. When it had finally become apparent that saving her pride wasn't worth losing Linc and the boys, she'd started the ball rolling toward moving lock, stock and barrel to a certain sprawling house outside of Duluth. He wanted to spend time with her? Well, she was going to give him all the time he could stand.

The first step had been to approach Karen and see if she wanted to buy out Chandra's half of the business. Karen had refused to consider severing their business relationship, suggesting that they adopt an alternative solution until Chandra was sure she wasn't coming back. "Don't burn the bridge till you've been safely on the other side so long the bridge looks rotten," she'd counseled sagely, as she'd come around her desk in a swish of crisp linen. The unflappable Karen Taylor had been completely confounded when Chandra asked her if she was part Indian and then burst out laughing.

"I'm sorry," Chandra had offered between guffaws. "It's just that I'd never noticed you spouting homespuns before." By the time Chandra had finished explaining about Henry, Karen had been laughing too.

With Chandra's business life settled, it had been a simple matter to arrange subletting her apartment. The building manager had a long waiting list of people who wanted a reasonably priced apartment within walking distance of Lake Michigan. That only left packing up her belongings.

Karen had barely entered Chandra's apartment Wednesday afternoon and seen all the cartons before demanding Chandra's car keys. Trusting that her friend had good intentions, Chandra turned them over. An hour later Karen returned with a U-Haul trailer attached to the back of Chandra's Audi.

Chandra admired a lot of things about her friend but had never appreciated her practical take-charge attitude more than she did during the rest of that day and the next. While Chandra continued to throw items in boxes and suitcases, Karen took inventory of Chandra's furniture and arranged to have it placed in storage, then pitched in to complete the packing. In the wee hours before dawn, Chandra climbed behind the wheel of her car and with complete confidence began the five-hundred-mile trip toward a lifetime of happiness.

That confidence didn't falter once during the long drive, nor after she'd arrived and explained her plan to Henry. It had been bolstered by the boys' enthusiastic welcome. But now, knowing that Linc was there and had probably already discovered all her worldly goods cluttering up his beautiful, serene bedroom, Chandra was beset with doubts. Her stomach was suddenly full of tight knots, her chest felt as if an anvil was resting on it and her mouth was bone-dry. She was about to put the keys back in the ignition and drive away when Henry plucked them from her hand and calmly got out of the car, striding to the door without looking back.

"Henry Raincloud, you'd better not be wrong," Chandra whispered softly to herself. The recipient of her implied threat had disappeared into the house but had symbolically left the door open behind him. Her feet felt weighted down as she dragged them up the flagstone walkway and mounted the first of the three steps leading onto the porch.

"You planning on a career change?" Linc's deep voice reached out to her from the doorway.

Chandra gripped the handrail a little tighter and swallowed hard. "Sort of."

There he was, the man she loved, casually leaning against the doorjamb, his arms crossed over his chest. Wearing a crisp white shirt and beautifully tailored charcoal trousers, he was more beautiful than any man had a right to be. Those incredible blue eyes bore into hers. The expression on his handsome face was unreadable.

Her heart was racing but her body wouldn't move. If she could have pried her hand loose from the railing, Chandra would have bolted back to the safety of her car. This wasn't the way it was supposed to go!

He should have given her a melting smile and rushed to scoop her into his arms, kissing her until she fainted. Of course, she should have been the one inside the house. She had planned to be composed, beautifully coiffed and elegantly garbed—not trudging up the steps on shaking legs, her hair a mass of wild curls and her body clad in shorts and a T-shirt.

"What exactly does 'sort of' mean?" he prodded, wincing when he saw the torment flickering across her features. He knew what she was planning but needed to hear it from her. This time, every word was for keeps.

"I should think it's obvious."

"Enlighten me," he demanded huskily, a soft glow in his eyes.

Seeing it, her white-knuckled grip relaxed and she stepped onto the edge of the porch. She forced herself to put one foot in front of the other and move toward him.

"Maybe I'm just slow, but I seem to be the only one around here who doesn't quite understand," he continued, stepping away from the door and meeting her halfway. "What does your moving in have to do with some old Chippewa custom?"

"I take it the boys must have said something about that." Chandra smiled when she received a nod of confirmation from Linc. "Actually it's the reverse of one."

Gathering courage from the amusement playing at the corners of his mouth, she looked him straight in the eye. There she saw all the encouragement she needed. He had no more forgotten about their love in the space of three weeks than she had. The elaborate tale she had concocted to gain entrance to his home was no longer necessary but she was going to play it out anyway. She'd spent a lot of time rehearsing this scenario and he was just going to have to bear with her. When she was finished, he wouldn't have a single doubt about her intentions.

She took a deep breath. "According to Henry, when a young warrior has proved his worth, he moves into his bride's wigwam and presents a feast to the parents of his chosen one. The couple are considered wed once the feast has been shared by the family of the intended."

Linc shoved his shaking hands into his pant

pockets to prevent them from reaching out for her. He rocked back and forth on the balls of his feet as he studied the planks of the porch. Listening to her dramatic speech, it was hard to keep from shouting out loud with unbridled joy. She'd gone to such lengths, he didn't have the heart to tell her it was all unnecessary. She loved giving speeches and he would be a most receptive audience.

"Just how is it that this particular warrior has proved. . .ah. . .her worth?" His eyes told her that he needed no more proof but was willing to listen if she wanted to offer some.

"This warrior has run the gauntlet for you and you know it," Chandra declared emphatically, then turned serious as she reminded him of all the tests she had passed. "First I had to prove to you that I like children—especially your children. Then I had to convince you that I do indeed love nature, that I could go camping and actually enjoy it."

"That's true," he conceded graciously.

"And now I'm even willing to compromise where my work is concerned. I'd never put my career before you and the boys."

"Oh, really?" Linc interrupted. Unable to resist touching her any longer, he tilted her chin up with the tip of his finger, then trailed that finger down her throat. "Where would you put it?"

"How about up in your bedroom?" Chandra managed breathlessly as his finger ran lightly along the deep U of her neckline. "I can set up an office there, establish a special branch of Collins and Taylor to handle small, local accounts and work out of our home."

"Hmm," Linc emitted thoughtfully. "Sounds pretty reasonable, especially the part about working in my bedroom. What else do you have to recommend yourself?" He began kissing the trail his fingers had made down her throat.

"Lincoln Young. You're driving me crazy," she croaked.

"It's only fair," he said in a gruff whisper and hauled her into his arms. "You've been driving me crazy for weeks." Before she could take a breath, his mouth covered hers, his kiss more fiery and possessive than any that had gone before.

"You forgot to mention how good you are at this," he said against her mouth, his hands roaming over the curves of her body, settling her into the hard planes of his. "I was insane to let you go. These past three weeks have taught me that love doesn't follow any time schedule. My heart knew that long before you left but my stubborn brain refused to accept it."

Chandra sagged against him. "Oh, Linc, does that mean you accept my proposal?"

Linc looped his hands together in the hollow of Chandra's back and rested his cheek on the top of her head. "By the sound of things, if I eat that dinner you've prepared, I'll have done more than accept a proposal."

Chandra leaned away from him, looking for and finding in his eyes all the love she wanted to see. "You certainly will have. You'll have married me and then you'll be stuck with me for life."

"Not quite." He grinned mysteriously. "I know a thing or two about Indian lore. I have an out."

"Oh you think so?" Chandra toyed with his necktie, sliding the loosened knot down a bit farther before slipping two more of his shirt buttons from their holes. She pressed her lips to the V of an exposed, very male chest, making a small damp circle on his skin. She felt a deep shudder ripple through his body and looked up in time to see him gulp. "What exactly is your 'out'?"

Linc had to clear his throat before answering. "The only requirement for divorce is that the couple cease to share the same wigwam."

"Mmm...Henry did say something about that." She raised up on her toes, pressed another kiss into his throat and slipped her hand inside his shirt. "But there's a little more to it than one of us moving out."

"And what's that?" Linc caught her wandering hand and stepped backward to escape the tantalizing touch of her lips. He was rapidly losing control, and if she kept up this torture any longer he was afraid he'd take her right there on the front porch in broad daylight.

"Any children have to be divided equally between the divorcing couple."

"But they're my children," he protested with exaggerated vehemence.

"Nope." Chandra shook her head vigorously. "Once you eat dinner, they're mine too. If you ever want a divorce, you'll have to split the children evenly with me. Since we have three, you'll just have to wait until a fourth arrives so we can divide them fairly."

She freed her hand from its imprisonment and slid it up around Linc's neck, urging his face back down to hers. "I love you, Lincoln Young." She punctuated

her statement with a kiss. "I love Ted. Chas. Matt.
Henry." Each name was followed with another kiss
but her lips lingered a little longer as she went down
through the list.

Linc's control was close to the breaking point and
he was not content to remain merely the receiver of
Chandra's final punctuation. He wanted to be a full
participant, escalating the simple statement to the
magnitude of a multiclaused exclamation. "I love you
too. Let's go upstairs and start proceedings," he suggested in a raw voice against her lips.

"Proceedings?" Chandra asked breathlessly.

Linc started backing across the porch, taking
Chandra with him as he inched along the planking.
"Let's get the fourth one started so I can get out of
this arranged marriage a little sooner." He nuzzled
her ear.

"Still might not be even," Chandra warned. She
shuffled her feet between his as he continued his
backward progress, her soft thigh brushing against
his hard groin with every movement. Linc's breathing was becoming more ragged with each step they
took.

"Might be a girl and we still wouldn't have an
equal split," Chandra suggested, halting their progress with a slow, drugging kiss.

"All the more reason to get started," Linc urged in
a strangled voice and started backing up again.

"How so?" Chandra twirled one fingertip around
the edge of Linc's ear and he groaned.

They made it to the doorway and started through
the hall. "If you're going for an equal settlement, and
the fourth one's a girl...." Linc's heel bumped

against the bottom step. "It's going to take quite a while to even things up so we'd better not waste any more time." He lifted Chandra into his arms and started mounting the stairs.

"Stop," Chandra whispered. "Henry and the boys."

Linc hesitated. "Don't hear anybody. They must have gone out the back door." He started up the stairs again.

"Lincoln, we don't need to do this until *after* the meal."

"So we anticipate the ceremony. Those chickens need to roast a while longer anyway. By my calculations we've got to come up with four girls and one more boy to square the numbers enough for an equitable settlement."

He took the remaining steps two at a time, made a fast turn at the landing and bolted up the second flight. "We can't afford to waste a single moment if we're ever going to get out of this marriage."

Chandra laughed, the warm sound echoing down the hallway. "Wouldn't it be easier just to skip dinner?"

"No!" Linc shouldered the bedroom door closed, pausing only long enough to lock it before striding across the room and dropping her very unceremoniously on the bed. His tie and shirt were on the floor before he made it to the wall of windows and yanked the drapes closed, and he was sliding his belt out of its loops by the time he reached the edge of the bed.

Seeing Chandra lying there watching him, he ordered with a sensual growl that sounded like the grating of bedsprings, "Get out of those clothes. Henry can't keep those boys out there forever."

Chandra reached for the hem of her knit top while she pushed at the heel of one shoe with the toe of the other. Shoes and clothes went sailing every which way. "I think I'm about to marry a wild man," Chandra mused as she watched Linc skim off his briefs. Her look of pure pleasure revealed just how much she was anticipating her life with said wild man.

"You'd better believe it, lady," Linc assured as he came down on the bed beside her. "A man so wildly in love with you he's going to explode into pieces if he has to wait any longer to have you."

No more words were necessary. Their bodies expressed all the longing and desire they had suffered during their separation. Holding himself in check, Linc worshiped every inch of Chandra, leaving no curve, no silken surface untouched before he joined their bodies and sent them on a wildly exciting journey to mindless oblivion.

Drifting in a pleasant mist of contentment, they lay side by side, their limbs limp across the wide bed. "I love you, Chandra." Linc's voice was hushed, reverent. He rolled to his side and leaned over her. "Will you share the winters of my life? Be the source of my wisdom, the beat of my heart? Will you be my wife and the mother to my children?"

Blinking tears, Chandra raised a shaky hand to curve gently over his cheek. "Our children," she corrected tenderly. "I thought you'd never ask."

Linc bent to kiss her but paused, sniffing the air. "Smells like your dinner is almost finished."

"How can you think of food at a time like this?" she queried in dismay.

"Not food, my love. Just wanted to get this ceremony over with and replenish our bodies enough so we'll have the strength to get to the county clerk's office Monday morning." He dropped a brief peck to her cheek and rolled off the bed.

Chandra's recovery from their lovemaking was a bit slower. Her mind was still hazy, her body suffused with a sweet exhaustion. "County clerk?"

"For a license," Linc supplied as he pulled on his pants and reached for his socks. "We can have another ceremony next week and then I figure with two ceremonies binding us together, plus all those kids we're going to have, it'll be pretty difficult for you to get out of this marriage."

"I'm not the one who brought up the escape clause," Chandra reminded him lightly as she dug in her suitcase for the dress she'd planned on wearing for the evening.

Linc tucked in his shirt, then came over to where Chandra knelt before her opened luggage. His teasing expression sobered as he gently pulled her to her feet. Very seriously he challenged, "Chandra, do you truly realize what you're getting into? Raising three children isn't all fishing or camping trips. You've only seen them on their best behavior. They fight. They cry. They misbehave and create havoc. Sometimes they get sick in the middle of the night. It's a big commitment."

"I realize that, Linc." Chandra's tone and expression were every bit as serious as his. "You adapted and so can I. You're not the only one who loves them. That very first day I met them, they stepped into my heart, turned around and sat down."

"You're really sure you've thought this through?"

"I certainly have. I'm an accountant, remember? I've spent a lot of time tallying up the credits and debits of this little company you've got here and I've decided it's a pretty sound investment." She smiled up at him, hoping to erase the serious lines around his face and mouth, but Linc wasn't ready to enjoy the humor in her analogy.

"I can't ask you to give up your career. You're a top notch C.P.A., and you've worked awfully hard to get where you are. Henry and I have been managing pretty well with the boys. I want you as my wife but not at the expense of your dreams. You don't have to alter your work that drastically for us. We can build our life around it."

"No, Linc, that's not the kind of marriage I want and neither do you. Even before I met you, I knew I didn't want to spend the rest of my life traveling between cities, spending most of my time in hotel rooms with only an occasional weekend at home."

Chandra started pulling on her dress as she talked. The pattern of muted pastel colors complemented her light olive skin and the soft fabric of the gathered skirt skimmed over her slender hips. The gold tones that swirled through the fabric were reflected in her rich chocolate eyes. Sunshine, Linc thought absently, before he returned his attention to her speech.

"Sooner or later, I would have made some kind of change in my work pattern even if you and the boys hadn't come into my life." She turned her back to Linc and he obediently zipped the dress for her. "Marrying you is the best reason in the world to make that change right now." She turned around and faced him. "I don't want our paths to merely cross now and then, Linc."

Chandra smoothed his shirtfront as she finished her speech. "I want to walk alongside you, sharing every day and every night."

Before Linc could find his voice and offer a reply, the peaceful quiet of the house was shattered by the banging of a door. Young voices and accompanying laughter carried up two flights of stairs, down a long hallway and through the closed door. "Hear that?" Linc asked, all his love shining from his eyes as he looked deeply into Chandra's soul.

"Those are the normal sounds around this house. This is your last chance to make an escape. Once you walk down those stairs and I eat that meal you've prepared, I'm holding you to an ironclad contract. You'll be part of this tribe forever."

Chandra locked her arms around his waist. "Let's go, I'm starving."